VANCE

AND

VANCE

RENEE JOINER

Oshun
Publications

Vance and Vance © Copyright 2020 by Renee Joiner

ISBN: 978-1-950378-49-4

Book design by Sabrina Watts

enchantedinkstudio.com

Published by Oshun Publications

www.oshunpublications.com

CONTENTS

Did you know you can take every story with you?

I know it's tough these days to simply find the time to relax and curl up with a good book. This is why I'm delighted to share that I have books available in audio book format.

Best of all, you can get the audio book version of any book by me for free as part of a 30-day Audible trial.

Members get free audio books every month and exclusive discounts. It's an excellent way to explore and determine if audio book learning works for you.

If you're not satisfied, you can cancel anytime within the trial period. You won't be charged, and you can even keep your audio book.

To choose a free audio book, click on your favorite title's cover to be taken to Audible's website for details.

Remember, there's no obligation to buy.

reneejoinerauthor.com/audiobooks

JOIN MY NEWSLETTER

GET UPDATES, FREEBIES & GIVEAWAYS

RENEEJOINERAUTHOR.COM/NEWSLETTER

SINGLES BY RENEE

Single Titles
Tempest
Half Demon
Wanted Undead or Alive
My Soul to Reap
Gravetide

ONE

V_{and}V

CLOSED BOOKS, UNFINISHED CHAPTERS

"Jenny is here to see you."

"Shit." Ariel Vance needed a bit more time to get her story straight, but it seemed as if they had all but run out of time. "Amy, could you please just keep her stalled for a few minutes?"

"Um, no. Listen, this woman looks about ready to skin her husband alive. Anyone unlucky enough to be around is going to be a casualty. I have a few different plans for my weekend."

Ariel raised an eyebrow. "You know I pay you for this type of thing, right?"

"I know. You also pay me, to be honest. Isn't that a non-negotiable quality when working for a detective agency? Speaking of, this chick's husband cheated on her. I kind of get that she wants to put up her deuces." Amy wasn't going to flinch. The worst thing about the best employees is that they know how to challenge their employers without over-stepping the bounds.

Ariel looked over at her sister. "You told her about the infidelity?"

Indya gave a sheepish, almost innocent look in return. "Well, yeah. Jenny is all fire and brimstone right now. I needed to give Amy a heads-up before she got burned."

"Urgh," Ariel groaned while massaging her temples in an attempt to plot her next move. "Fine. Where is she now?"

"In your office, having a coffee," Amy replied.

"Oh, well isn't that nice. Did you remember the biscotti?" Ariel asked half-irritated.

"Mhmm, no. We're fresh out, hun. I did put the A/C on, though. She needed to cool down."

The phone rang before Ariel could offer a retort, and Amy picked up the receiver.

Sighing, she signaled for her sister to follow, and they headed to her office. Jenny was sitting at the desk, visibly trying to control herself as a trembling hand brought the coffee cup to her lips. Indya didn't have to read her thoughts to know she was apprehensive. So instead, her sister took the lead.

"Well, Jenny, we have your case file right here. Are you ready to hear—?"

"—what that worthless ingrate did?" Jenny said, finishing her sentence. "Fuck, yes." She nearly fell out of the chair as she swiped to grab the docket, whipping out the evidence of the last few days. Her eyes jumped from photo to photo, running through one report after the other, as she soaked in one fraction of what was possibly two years of infidelity by her husband. Ariel had never seen a woman's eyes turn from fire to ice, but she definitely didn't want to be in Jenny's soon-to-be-ex's shoes. "So, you read him properly, didn't you?"

"Like a book," Indya answered. "He had a few slips of the tongue when we were looking for a motive to use spyware—when we approached him in disguise. After that, technology was pretty much on our side."

Jenny slammed the case docket shut. "So, when do we take the camera crew to go and confront him?"

Ariel nearly choked on the laugh she wanted to suppress. "Uh, Jenny. This isn't Cheaters. We stay out of the aftermath of our findings. Although, I am sure that whatever you are about to unleash on him would be worthy of late-night reality viewing."

Jenny's look was deadpan as she chucked down the last of her piping hot coffee and flamboyantly flung her handbag over her shoulder. "Well, ladies, I wish I could say it has been a pleasure, but I have a reprobate of a spouse to deal with. Judging by the evidence, he should be bringing his little hussy home in about half an hour. I have a climax to ruin." With that, she stepped out and charged back through the office.

Indya was the first to say something. "Did she just say?"

"Yup. I envy the fly on the wall to that little confrontation."

Indya sagged in the chair. "Well, that is case five in three weeks. I'm exhausted."

"Yeah, me too. The agency has been doing well. I think we can finally take a break."

Indya sat back in the office chair, contemplating a bit as a far-away look crossed her face. Ariel knew precisely what it meant.

"Oh, God. I know that face. You're not planning on taking a break at all, are you?"

"I was. Then I started thinking of the cases we never solved. Or, rather, the ones we never have time for." Indya returned her eyes to meet Ariel's, and there was just enough emotion there that Ariel immediately shut down.

"Absolutely not."

Indya jumped up and leaned over the desk with an almost pleading look to her sister. "Come on, El. You can't seriously tell me you never wondered what happened to them."

"I wonder about a great many things, but playing with hypotheticals has always gotten me into dark places," Ariel answered.

"God. Do you have to be so dismissive? Listen. I have been thinking of a new angle by which to approach this. We just need—"

"No! Indya, you have to let go. Mom and Dad are gone. Looking for them isn't going to bring them back!" Ariel's tone was a bit harsher than she intended, but she had been down this road before. It never ended well.

Indya flinched only slightly at her sister's backlash before giving a calm and measured answer. "Perhaps they never left. Maybe you just haven't looked hard enough. You've given up every time."

Ariel's eyes flashed with anger. "That is unfair, and you know—"

"Take your break," Indya interrupted, "it's fine. By all means. Call me when you're ready for the next case." With that, she stormed out, leaving Ariel flabbergasted as to how things had escalated in a matter of a few minutes. She didn't have much time to be taken aback, however. She had a date to prepare for. She just hoped she'd be able to enjoy it now.

THE WINE WAS LIKE VELVET, its touch a seduction on the palate. It perfectly rounded off the taste of their meal. "God, that's some good vino."

"Clearly. You've been admiring the vintage more than you have me," Jaydon teased.

Ariel raised her eyes to peek ever so playfully beneath her lashes. "Well, some men improve with age, and I do like my men the way I like my wine. You'll get there, babe."

He gave a mischievous little smirk before he cut into his steak. Somehow, he had the talent of doing everything with suave. Jaydon was a walking temptation. Ariel often wondered whether it was the reason for her attraction to him—or the fact that she couldn't get a read on him. "Seems like you needed it."

"It's just good to unwind a bit." She took another sip and closed her eyes involuntarily as the heady flavors played on her tongue.

"What's happening at the detective agency these days?" Jaydon asked, taking a sip from his own glass.

"It's been busy. We've had a weird bunch of cases of late. Money laundering, attempted homicide, unfaithful—and unfortunate—husbands," she answered, raising an eyebrow in mock challenge as she forked a piece of tender meat.

Jaydon sat back, returning her look. "What makes him unfortunate?"

"A smart woman," she said, smiling, before raising her glass to her lips.

"Ah, I see. Some men would consider themselves lucky to have that."

"Of course. You should know." She winked at him.

His mouth curled into one of those famously ambiguous smiles. Jaydon was one of those rare people whose expressions could mean a hundred different things, even if the occasion remained the same. It drove her a little nuts. She and her sister counted themselves as experts in finding out what made people tick. Yet, she had to put the puzzle that was her boyfriend together piece by piece—like the average girl on the block. Her grandmother had also joked that men were ridiculously simple to unravel—trust her, be a detective, and find the Rubik's Cube among the bunch.

"You're doing it again," she stated, blushing ever so slightly against her will.

"Looking at you? Can you blame me?" he asked.

Before she could respond, his phone rang. That handsome smile melted away, and his face turned almost serious. Reaching into his pocket, he drew out the ringing device. With one look at the screen, his eyes sparkled in recognition before he apologized, "Sorry, babe, I need to take this." He stood up from the table and stalked off toward the restaurant's entrance, answering the call in a hushed tone.

Ariel frowned, thinking that his reaction was slightly off. Yet, she didn't overthink it, instead deciding to survey the crowded restaurant. The Butcher's Boudoir was packed that night, and she found entertainment by watching people at the other tables. It wasn't long until Jaydon returned. She looked up as he approached and knew almost immediately that he was not about to stay. "You're leaving, aren't you?"

"I'm sorry. I got an urgent call from work. Listen, I feel like crap. I promise to make it up to you. Okay?" He walked around to her side of the table, knelt down, and then cupped her hands as he looked into her eyes. "You know I love you, right?" He leaned forward, giving her a kiss before he stood and then left.

Ariel didn't know how long she sat there, unable to move after he had gone. He had never said that before. Love. There was no emotion-laden precursor to the confession. He said it almost as if she should have known it all along. It caught her completely off guard. Perhaps it was because she wasn't quite sure if she felt as strongly about him in return.

Suddenly, another feeling dominated her. It was enough to take her mind off what Jaydon had said. She wasn't sure what it was, but it was making her uneasy. She put down her glass and started rummaging through her bag until she found her own phone.

TWO

V_{and}V

THE SLEUTH

"There is a dial pad on the lock. I need a code from you."

"Give me a sec. There's a spicy firewall entrenched in the security system. I need to douse it."

"Drench it, and hurry! I hear footsteps coming."

"You're going to have to improvise. Better draw on some of those skills."

"Dammit!" Indya pulled the side-part of her hair over her ear to cover the receiver through which Zoe was talking. She flipped her satchel forward just as a security guard came around the corner. Falling into character, she made as if she was digging through her bag, looking for something.

"Everything alright, miss? We are about to close the building."

She looked up in surprise, pretending she was noticing him for the first time. Her eyes lingered on his nametag for a split second before she met his eyes. "Oh, man, Sean. I feel like such an idiot. I left my phone in the server room, and as I was looking for my keycard, I realized I left it inside as well."

Sean smiled. Even if he didn't know who she was, he

certainly looked flattered by the fact that she seemed to know his name. "That's some bad luck. Luckily I came around. Hey, you're the new technician, aren't you?"

Zoe's intel was on point. The new job opening in the company was the perfect alibi. "Yeah, I'm still learning my way around this place and this crazy intricate system. You'd think a tech native like me would know my way around digital access."

"Well, it should be no problem. You just need to punch in the security bypass code."

Shit. Indya needed to think quickly. Her sidekick still hadn't buzzed in with the code. Elitelligence was proving unhackable on every front. They couldn't even penetrate the outer edges of its security. "The bypass code Oh right, I think I wrote it down somewhere. I should really memorize it," she laughed. She started rummaging through the bag again, keeping herself from breaking out in a nervous sweat. She was pretty deep inside the building. If she was discovered trespassing, it wouldn't be taken as accidental.

After a while, Sean relieved her of her misery. "Hey, no sweat." He took out his keycard and held it in front of the dial pad scanner. After a second, the lock disengaged, and the guard opened the door. "There you go. You can go ahead and run in. I'm going to have a look through the rest of the place before I engage the alarm. Can you show yourself out?"

"Sure. Thanks, Sean." She winked at him, and he blushed before dashing off. She was lucky this time. Luckily Sean was craving some affirmation. She could tell.

"You practically seduced him without even realizing it, didn't you?" Zoe commented in her ear.

"I can play the damsel in distress if I need to," Indya answered through the microphone hidden in her collar before closing the door behind her. "Well, since you didn't dig up access codes, I hope you've been using the time to program this fly I'm supposed to plant on the wall."

"Just about there. I need you to make your way to the UPS. It will be right underneath the station equipped with the power management software."

"You want to tamper with the power supply?"

"The device you have will short-circuit the battery backup. If I can dip the power, which means the servers will shut down before restarting. The firewall will drop for a while, giving me enough time to bypass it and get inside the servers by the time they fire up again."

Indya walked among the racks and enclosure until she found the station. "Are you telling me you've hijacked the building's electrical grid?"

"It's not my fault; they automated it."

Reaching into her pocket, Indya withdrew the small electronic disc that fits inside her palm. "Where exactly do you need me to plant it?"

"As close to the power management station as possible. Listen, once I work my magic, the blackout will raise the alarm. I need you to get out of there right away."

Her words weren't even cold before Indya heard the door to the server room opening.

She ducked before cursing. "Fuck! Someone just came in. I haven't even planted it."

"I suggest you do. It's magnetic, so it will give me the range I need to upset the system. Smash it on the side panel, and skulk out of there, bitch!"

Indya did just that and threw herself against the server units on the opposite side. The spacious room was large and dark enough to hide in, but only if she had a position on her enemy. What she found odd was that she couldn't get a read on the new visitor's mind. She slid along the racks and occasionally looked through the slats between the server boxes. Reaching the end of the row, she peeked around a corner to see a figure emerge from the far side.

She caught her breath and ducked back. "What the hell?"

"Who's the predator on your trail?"

"It's Jaydon."

"Your sister's guy? What's he doing t—?"

"I don't know. His mind is blocked. I'll have to sneak out of here by instinct alone."

"Give me a sec."

Indya listened, waiting intently on Jaydon's footsteps. As he got closer to her position more than once, it was all she could do to meld to the shadows and slip around corners at precisely the right moments. It felt like Zoe was taking forever, but after a minute, she chimed back in.

"Sorry. I'm back."

"God! What took you? This guy is like a bloodhound," Indya whispered furiously.

"This system is really pesky. You have no idea. But, I managed to access a building schematic. If you can snake your way back past the UPS, then you'll find a fire escape that leads down and out."

"He's sniffing around awfully close to that area. I'll need a distraction."

"Coming up," Zoe said. "Think fast."

The entire room shut down, and Indya didn't hesitate. With footfalls softer than a leopard's footsteps, she dashed among the shelves and reached the now unlocked escape just as she heard a figure shuffling one shelf over. She slipped through the door and closed it behind her.

She exhaled just as the building's power surged alive,

and the lights flickered back on. Through the door, she heard new arrivals. Among them, she could make out Sean's anxious voice as he interacted with Jaydon. Most of their conversation was muffled, but as they passed the fire escape, Indya heard his firm instruction to lock down the place. Their voices receded, and as she was about to check in with Zoe, she felt her phone vibrate.

The sensation made her jump, and she cursed under her breath before taking out her phone to see who was calling. It was her sister.

"Dammit," she whispered to herself, weighing the decision to answer or not. She knows something is up, Indya thought, which means she's only going to grow more suspicious if I ignore the call. She hesitated a second longer before answering. "Ariel, I can't really talk right now."

"Why? Something's wrong, isn't it? I sense it, even if I can't get a feeling for the shape of your thoughts right now."

"Our last conversation didn't exactly go great. Of course, you'd think something is off."

"Don't be dismissive Indie," Ariel responded, almost sounding hurt, "I'm only worried that—"

"Listen," Indya interrupted, "I'll check in later. Now is really not a great time. Don't worry about me. I promise we'll talk this out." She stayed on the line long enough to hear Ariel forming the start of a response before she hung up.

"Sibling quarrels?" Zoe said her voice firing back through the receiver.

"Yeah, and I have a feeling it isn't over either. Her boyfriend has become an unexpected role player in this. We'll need to dig up all the dirt we can on him. You managed to get deeper into their systems?"

"It was a gnarly one, but I'm on the other side," Zoe

answered. "Tell you what; you get out of there and head on back. Check your watch for a building map. I'll get working and have some info by the time you return. You need to hurry, though. From what I can see, that shy guard is pretty quick on implementing the lockdown."

Indya pounded down the stairwell while answering, "Next time, I'm going to be in your ear, prompting you with nonchalant warnings to move your ass while trying to maintain stealth."

"That's nice. I'll let you have a shot at hacking once you can finally figure out how to download free antivirus trials. Baby steps."

Respectable tech support is so hard to come by, Indya thought, as she made her way out of the building.

THREE

V and V

COLD CASE

"He said what?" Amy asked, dropping the receiver of the reception phone while barely able to contain her excitement. On the other end of the line, Ariel could hear as the confused caller was trying to get the attention of an absent ear.

"Um, why don't you sign off with the caller first," Ariel suggested.

Giving the receiver a disinterested glance, she picked it up a second and simply put it down to end the call.

"Amy!"

"Oh, whatever. It's just that scumbag that cheated on your last client. He approached the agency to get some dirt on his little side hussy that's run away with some of his fortune. The deceiver got deceived. Let's talk about relationships that are actually working out!"

"We still have an operation to run here, you know. Between 9 and 5 we—"

"Find more than enough time to solve cases while talking about the crap in our personal lives. Honey, I have an entire list of potential case files for you to pick from.

Business is good. Now, stop changing the topic, will you? A man just confessed his undying love to you!" Amy was channeling her signature melodrama.

"Honestly, that's taking it a bit far. Undying? That's some serious embellishment," Ariel said, looking skeptical.

"Look, if we don't embellish the things that a man says every now and then, then they turn out to be pretty boring," Amy offered in response.

"What's this about boring men?" It was Indya. She walked around her sister, leaning on the reception counter as she regarded both women.

Ariel was caught off guard. She didn't know if she was still reeling from Jaydon's confession last night, but she was surprised that she didn't sense her sister's approach. "Where've you been all morning?" she asked.

"Sleeping in. Had a rough night."

"Did yours involve a man as well?"

Indya looked confused about a response, but Ariel noticed as recognition dawned on her face—probably from reading Amy's palpable excitement. "Oh, right. Ariel had a date last night. How did that go?" There was an edge to her tone that piqued Ariel's attention. It was a little more than mild or innocent interest, but she wasn't yet sure how to label it.

"From the sound of it," Amy started, "the two kids had the perfect setting for a heartfelt moment. Good food, drink, ambiance. No wonder he told her he loved her."

Indya raised an eyebrow. "Whoa. Well, you must have felt a certain kind of way about that?"

"That's one way of putting it," Ariel answered. "Anyway, Amy, you still have that list?"

Amy slid the list toward her. "From now on, I want

updates on the daily. I am hinging all my romantic fantasies on the vicarious experience of your love life."

"Yes, ma'am." Ariel answered sarcastically. "Let me know if I can answer the calls as well, to save you time for daydreaming."

Amy rolled her eyes and answered another incoming call, right on cue. Ariel turned to her sister, nodding toward her office. They both headed in that direction, and after closing the door behind them, the sisters made the same statement in unison, "We need to talk."

Neither of them was really surprised. Indya was the first to follow up with a question. "How much do you really know about Jaydon?"

"O-K. I didn't really expect that" answered Ariel.

"Don't you find it odd that neither of us can read him?" Indya prodded relentlessly.

Ariel didn't know if she was taken aback or entirely dumbfounded by the sudden line of questioning. A part of her felt glad that her sister was suddenly preoccupied with something else besides their parents, but she just wished it wasn't her boyfriend. "I find many things odd, like your sudden interest in him. You seem pretty unmindful of him for the most part."

There was a moment, just a moment when she noticed how her sister was looking for the right response. After a few seconds, she answered, "Well, if he did tell you he loves you, and then I guess it is my right to engage in a little interrogation. He obviously has intentions."

"And what are your intentions? Why are you so interested in my dating life all of a sudden?"

"You're avoiding the question," Indya countered.

Ariel sighed, "I haven't really wrapped my mind around

what those intentions are. I don't know my own, to be quite frank."

Indya gave her sister a stern look before responding. "That's the thing, though. We are used to wrapping our minds around what other people want. It's strange to come across someone where that's not the case. Predictability offers certainty, El. If someone keeps you wondering—"

"Then you become more authentic," Ariel said, cutting her off. "Look, this is still new. I like Jaydon because he is not predictable, and I always found that exciting, I guess. Right now, I'm just facing one of those ambivalent scenarios where I can't really figure out what I'm supposed to feel."

Indya cocked her head to the side, "It seems simple to me, actually. If someone says they love you, should you not feel the s—?"

"Indya!" Ariel interjected, knowing where her sister was going with this. "I just want to get my mind on a case. I know I said I wanted a break, but I think I need to get back in the groove of a mystery. And not one about my personal life."

Indya threw her hands up in surrender. "Fine, fine." Ariel's desk was piled with fresh case dockets. It was likely that Amy got them ready before handing her the list this morning. Grabbing the top one, Indya plunked down in the visitor's chair and started paging through the file on the very top.

Watching her sister a moment longer, Ariel did the same, taking the next one. At first, her glimpses through the case details were nothing but a passive gesture, until further perusal revealed that it was built around a missing father. Suddenly, she felt intently engaged with the story. Against her will, the death of their parents started skulking in the back of her mind. Perhaps this is what her sister felt, but she could not be sure. As she continued reading, she was tempted to pick up the case.

"Anything?"

"I am afraid to get excited, but this may—"

A photo fell from the docket as she turned the page. Picking it up, Ariel drew her breath in rapidly as she looked at her father's distantly familiar features.

FOUR

V~and~V

BREADCRUMBS

Indya was pacing, rereading the file for what must have been the fifth time. Her laptop was out, and she was researching what she could between spurts of reviewing the same information. She only had a handful of clues by which she could pick up the trail. It was making her frantic, and she must have appeared visibly upset to Ariel. She was sure her sister was by no means unfazed by the findings, but she wanted more of a reaction out of her."

"Indya, I think you need to calm down."

"A picture of our father just randomly fell from a case file. No offense, but that is the worst damn thing you can say to me right now."

"Look, I'm not trying to vex you. But right now, more than ever, keeping a cool head is key if you want to get any closer to the truth," Ariel explained.

"Do you? Do you want to get closer to the truth?" Indya challenged, perhaps a tad too harshly.

Ariel only flinched a second before becoming reactive. "Of course, I do! What kind of question is that? I saw his face, the same as you. I felt the same things you did. I just know how to be rational, something you sorely need to adopt in your life."

Indya was hardly processing her sister's caution. She paged back through the file, tracing her finger down the lines in search of something she read. "There. This date bugs the hell out of me. This man's records only start a few weeks after our parents' accident. Everything before that seems nonexistent."

"That doesn't necessarily imply—"

"Ariel, it implies a hell of a fucking lot. Whose background check starts at that point in time? This man," she started, furiously tapping at the picture between them, "has a history. I think it's a history he wanted to hide."

Suddenly there was a knock. Their heads whipped around in the direction of the sound. Ariel composed herself, standing up to open the door. Jaydon stood on the other side. "Hey girls," he greeted them amiably before leaning down to kiss Ariel on the cheek.

Of course, he would show up, Indya thought. She immediately felt herself go stiff. He had been at the security company she snuck into last night. Even though her evasion of him was successful, his presence nonetheless unnerved her. Indya forced a smile and nodded in acknowledgment. Ariel was far better at being the great pretender when it came to personal situations. It was ironic because a lot of Indya's vigilante work required her to assume many faces, but she was not as skilled.

"Hey um, what are you doing here?" Ariel asked. She was blushing, and there was a discomfort just under the surface of the façade she assumed. Maybe Jaydon didn't notice, but it didn't escape Indya's attention.

"Well, I left in such a hurry last night; I thought I could take you out for breakfast."

"Uh it's like 11:30," Ariel responded. "And I'm kind of—"

"An early lunch then," he interrupted. "C'mon. I won't keep you long."

Amy popped her head around the corner at just that moment. She looked about ready to say something urgently before noticing Jaydon. The familiar gleam of mischief filled her eye. "Well, hello. Haven't seen you in these halls in ages," she said, feigning surprise and mild flirtation.

Typical, Indya thought. She probably charged into the scanning room just as he came in just so she could have a 'chance' encounter in her boss's office. Indya had managed to figure out Amy reasonably quickly in the time she had worked for them. There was never a dull moment with her around. She could gift-wrap the dreariest day in drama. Above that, her investment in the scintillating stories of other's lives was more apparent than her work ethic.

"I can't always be barging in on a bunch of formidable women exacting fine justice."

Oh God, Indya thought, he's one of those prone to disingenuous misogynist compliments.

"Well, honey, you know we can multitask," Amy responded, winking at him.

Ariel cleared her throat. "You looked like you were about to tell me something important?"

Ooh, that was almost bitchy. Indya had to force down a smile.

"Right, right," Amy said, snapping back from her fantasy, "I need you to come deal with something. Remember, Zimmerman?"

Ariel's eyes widened. "Shit!" She turned to Jaydon. "I'll be right back." She dashed off, dragging Amy along. Indya was left alone with Jaydon in the room.

"What the hell is Zimmerman?"

"Don't ask. That case has always been her personal little train wreck. I don't even know everything about it." She took her seat in one of Ariel's office chairs. "So, how have things been between the two of you?"

There was a moment of hesitation Indya wished had lasted longer. Still, he responded before she could get a good read on him. "Smooth sailing. I'm crazy about her, obviously, but I have an idea that fact already made the rounds this morning."

Indya felt like she had a foot lodged into her mouth.

"Relax. Knowing Amy, she probably interrogated your sister into telling her everything this morning. She is a vicarious romantic."

He was good, too good. Not only was he throwing up a mental block, but he was reading the room like a pro. "Well, you dropped quite the bomb last night," she said, keeping her tone good-natured. "Is it any surprise the shockwaves are still being felt?"

"I've always liked to be upfront about things. Honesty gets us to where we need to be a whole lot quicker," he said, looking her straight in the eye.

His last words were almost haunting. It was the kind of statement that had the potential to come back to you much later when you least expected it. No matter how hard she tried, she couldn't read his mind. He was as closed off to her as he had been the night before. When she was sneaking around the company. Was he running it? She wondered. It was almost as if he was purposefully blocking her, aware of what she was trying to do. It made her wonder if he knew that she was the one in the server room the previous night. The thought made her tense, even more so in the full force of the look he threw her way. That was enough of a cue for her to get out.

"Well, I bet Ariel will be back soon. I have to go and investigate a lead. I'll see you around."

"Keep well now. Try and stay out of trouble."

Depends on whether you keep yourself out of it, she thought. "I'll try." She headed out, feeling her muscles unwind once she left the room.

Exiting the office, her fingers worked nimbly to enter the unlock sequence on her watch so she could establish a connection between the device and her audio bud. Zoe's voice came through.

"What's up?"

"I need you to check an address for me."

HALF AN HOUR LATER, she was sitting underneath a veranda in the back garden of a swanky manor. It was in a suburban area near the city center. It had been easy enough to get the guard at the gate to allow her in. She had thought the challenge would come in talking to the mistress of the mansion.

As she explained her presence to the person who answered the door, the woman stood at the top of the stairwell. She heralded Indya's visit as if she was god sent, instructing the man to show Indya outside, where she would be joining her shortly. She also called for some refreshments to be prepared.

The next thing Indya knew, she was sipping on a gin and tonic while staring at a spread of luncheon snacks that looked as if it had been freshly prepared by a wedding caterer. Well, it is a Saturday, she thought. Indulgences could be allowed. "Mrs. Thompson, this is all completely unnecessary."

"Nonsense. I see no sense in talking business without some manner by which to swallow down a tough conversation. Please, help yourself." She sat back in her chair and closed her eyes before gulping down nearly half of her own drink. Placing the glass back on the table in front of her, she caught Indya staring. "For the nerves, dear. Now, you are here to talk about my husband and the case I opened in light of his disappearance."

"Yes." Deciding she might as well surrender to the moment, she took a sip of her own drink and took out her recorder.

"Aren't we comfortable." It was Zoe. Indya had asked for her intel to be in her ear the entire time. That meant that she'd have to endure any snarky comments that came through. She needed her, though. Whatever information this woman was going to convey, Zoe could look up and investigate in real-time. The recorder was merely for show.

"I noticed that there were some photographs in the hallway of your husband accepting awards, but I could not read the inscriptions on the plaques"

"It was in recognition of the work he did. He was part of many collaborative projects with the BBS."

"Bureau of Biogenic Sciences. They have been in the news a lot of late," Indya responded.

"Because of the work he did, no doubt," Mrs. Thompson responded with a sense of pride. "He crossed boundaries that those other charlatans were too afraid of venturing into." She picked up her drink again. "He was obsessed. They referred to him as the benevolent Hitler."

Indya raised an eyebrow in interest. "That is quite the title."

"No wonder," Zoe chimed in through the earpiece, "From what I can see, this man was heavily involved in bioengineering. Keywords like 'super race' are popping up."

Addressing Mrs. Thompson, Indya said, "From the way you put it, it seemed like he applied his knowledge to improve people on a biological level."

"And he was making strides in his work." Her emphasis on the word was one of the many telltale signs of the wife's admiration for her brilliant husband. "But more importantly, what you should be noting is that he may have been kidnapped because of it"

"Kidnapped! But—"

"Sorry dear, I need to highlight this: I just can't discard the fact that you bear a striking resemblance to him. It's in the eyes, grey as an approaching storm. Maybe it's the strong jawline or the fierce expression that just seems permanently impressed on your features—regardless of the emotion. He also had dark hair when he was in his mid-20s."

The sudden change of topic forced Indya to slow her line of questioning, despite the new information. "I guess my features are common enough."

Mrs. Thompson didn't buy it. She merely nodded as if considering the response before she sat back again. "It must be a shock. There was another woman at your agency that left me with the same impression when I opened the case."

She might as well have thrown a grenade in Indya's face. "Wait, what?"

"God, this is about to get really juicy," Zoe said, audibly typing away on her end of the transmission.

"SHE WENT OFF ON HER OWN?" Ariel asked, stunned.

"Well, yeah. Wasn't she supposed to?" Jaydon asked. "I didn't see anyone leaving with her."

Ariel fell in the chair behind her desk, massaging her temples. "My sister has a will of her own. I actually didn't expect anything less. We're both stubborn and persistent. It just manifested differently. She'll be fine. She is doing some foundational work for this new case we are hot on the trail of." She'll be okay, Ariel reassured herself. If anything goes south, she was sure her sister would send a psychic wave to alert her of trouble. Indya just had the unique predisposition of getting into it at the most inopportune times.

Jaydon was interested. "What kind of case have you got on your hands?"

"Just research and tracking." She couldn't reveal too much to him, despite him being her boyfriend. They were still a professional detective agency. Besides, the personal investment they both had was something she wanted to keep concealed for the time being. "So, where exactly did you head off to in such a hurry last night?"

"Someone wormed their way into the building where we're based without leaving much of a trail. As head of security, I needed to check it out."

"Would the break-in not have alerted the guards immediately?" Ariel asked.

"It wasn't really a break-in. There was no forced entry. It was more of a security breach and then unprohibited access to the building's resources. We only picked up on it after a delayed alarm response. They were good, whoever they are. Though, we couldn't figure out what they were after."

"Man. Sounds like they hacked the system."

"Or had help doing it," he offered. "Speaking of help. If this new investigation involves tracking, I have a few contacts that could really help find whoever needs finding. Work is pretty tight on my end, but if we work together on something, I might see more of you. It would be great to be more involved in this side of your life."

Ariel was quiet for a moment before answering, "Thank you. I'll keep that in mind once we know a bit more." Perhaps she should have said something more to have made the response less mechanical. Still, it only allowed the confusion of the previous night to resurface. She found it silly that the word 'love' could frazzle her so, but perhaps she was struggling to accept the genuineness thereof. Neither of them had mentioned last night again, and she wondered if he genuinely even meant what he had said. She confessed to none of these thoughts. She simply met his eyes as he looked at her, perhaps delving for some kind of mirrored emotion.

He leaned forward then and kissed her forehead. "You seem pretty busy. We can reschedule instead. I'm glad I came to see you, though." He made to leave, and just as he was about to walk through the door, he stopped and turned to her one last time. "I can see you're guarded, and that's okay. I told you last night before leaving was genuine, but I don't expect you to immediately feel the same. Just know you can count on me, okay?" He winked, offered a warm smile, and then turned the corner.

Ariel gave a heavy sigh, collecting her disparate feelings into one place where she could make sense of them. "Why is this such a big deal?" she asked out loud.

She nearly fell out of her chair as a figure came rushing in, catching herself on the doorframe. It was Indya.

"Jesus! You know, our twin telepathy isn't that great! Don't you ever call?"

Indya was almost panting. Whether it was from excitement or her rushing here, Ariel was unsure. "Clearly, we need to sync ourselves better then; because boy do I have news for you!"

"Well, close the—"

Indya was one step ahead of her. She slammed the door shut before racing to the desk to plant the recorder on Ariel's desk. She tampered with the settings a bit, and after a while, she hit play. The stored file came to life.

"...he believed he could create the next generation of super humans. It was idealistic, daring, and ultimately it could spell his downfall"

Indya pressed the pause button and looked her sister straight in the eye. "The missing guy from the file—a.k.a. dad—was experimenting with altering human genomes to display unique characteristics. He was a bioengineer—a scientist who had garnered accolades in the last few years with his crazy ideas and wild experiments. Ever wondered why we've heard about the biomedical science institute so much? This is why!"

"Whoa! Okay, slow down." Ariel simply stared at her sister. "Let's just backtrack: Bioengineering? Alright dad was a professor of bioengineering, but he was purely academic. He hated the corporate agenda that was fueling research beyond the altruistic cause of expanding knowledge. Didn't he? Why would he covet the attention of science institutes? This doesn't sound like the same man."

"El, people hardly have one face. We should know that

better than anyone. People's intentions don't always align with the roles they play."

"How did you—wait, did you go see his wife?" Ariel asked.

"Um, yeah. How did you think I got hold of all this info? Besides, why are you surprised? From what I could gather, the two of you already had your turn-in meeting." The statement was almost accusatory, but Ariel didn't know what her crime was. Indya saw her perplexed reaction and seemed to mirror her confusion, albeit for different reasons. "Wait, didn't you?"

"No. You saw my reaction when I first found his picture in the file. It was—" Ariel stopped short. As if she'd realized something. "Unless we did meet. There was a woman who came in weeks ago to open a case. I started documenting some of the info but had to give it over to Amy when I was dealing with the Zimmerman fiasco. She must have handled all the details and evidence that would have put me on the scent of this trail weeks ago—when it was still fresh. Dammit!"

"Sorry, I didn't mean to—" Indya started, unsure of how best to apologize. "Listen, we're on the case now, so it's fine. We'll fire up every scrap of evidence we can."

Ariel's mind was far away. She was staring vacantly at space and thought out loud. "Why would he fake his own death? Why would he remarry and start a new life? There are just too many unanswered questions. God, he even has a kid."

Indya must have seen the effect this was having on her. She recognized it, going through spurts of it often herself. Only then she didn't have any semblance of an answer. "Luckily, we are in the right kind of business to start answering them."

"We've spent so much of our lives obsessing about this already." She looked down at her feet, her own thoughts filling the silence as the call to action became ever more apparent. "But perhaps we have been going into this too blindly. Now that we have a lead, perhaps it's time to throw the deer into some headlights."

V_{and}V

THE HUNT

The Storm Den, the latest among a revolving list of names by which Zoe referred to their secret base of operations, was a cavernous subterranean playroom of the newest espionage technology. All totally illegitimately acquired or a complete novelty in their own right. She came upon the idea when she started to refer to the city's law enforcement as a pack of brutish wolves that tore crime apart at their leisure. It left the leftovers of injustice out there, completely unresolved, for the more cunning to pick up the trail. Indya still wasn't sure about the name, The Vixen, which Zoe had bestowed on her. She said it sounded sexy.

Either way, she rolled with it. As long as the job got done.

It was already 23:00 as she walked into The Den, and she found Zoe staring at one of the monitors with several files opened.

"Still researching BBS? I see you have their records pulled up."

"It's crazy. The company has breached many ethical

codes of late, and these are only the most recent records—personal researcher accounts. They weren't even reported on. I haven't even penetrated the surface of their database, and their hands are already pretty bloody. How did anyone miss all this? The news was pretty scant on the details, that's for sure."

Indya folded her arms as she scanned across bits of the displayed records. "Investors, capitalists, crazed scientists judging from my father's new digs during his time spent posing as Sean Thompson; I can bet you that a lot of money was pushed in to keep a lot of their experiments under wraps. They'll still be scrambling around to dodge some media coverage from what his wife told me today. I think we can start biting at their ankles without them paying too much attention to us."

Zoe swung around, clearly surprised by her proposal. "You want to infiltrate the institute? You just found out about them today."

"I respond to the heat when the fire is stoked," Indya answered.

"God, aren't you tired? Listen bitch, you're tough as nails. I know you can heal and recover fast and all, but I literally haven't seen you close your eyes for more than two hours at night."

"Being nocturnal is but one of my many superpowers. But hey, if you're tired, I understand. Just outfit me with some tech and—"

"Are you kidding?" Zoe said, clearly excited. "I'm definitely not letting you have all the fun. There are some field gadgets that I would love to try out myself. I'm tagging along for this one. Besides, remote IT backup isn't going to cut it with this mission. Neither is your knack for reading people.

The institute's security system is almost completely automated, just like Elitelligence. You need hard support right at your back, along with some old-school stealth."

"Well then, I see no reason why we're still sitting here discussing it. Are you ready to gear up?"

ANYONE LOOKING at Zoe might have easily discounted her worth in the field. She was a tiny thing that you would more than likely label as the bookish type. Although she had a wicked talent for finding and processing information, she was by no means the shy or reclusive type. She was an explosive ball of energy that had no problem matching the grace and stamina by which Indya made her way through dangerous territory. By being a tech whiz on top of it all, she was a double threat that could steal the best field agent's thunder.

Breaking through the first line of building security was easy enough. The building's side was a dedicated cargo bay where supplies, specimens, and equipment were in a constant exchange game as shipments arrived and were sent off. Due to the broad scope of their research, the BBS operated nearly 24/7 to disseminate new findings. It was the only breach in the outer security since it hinged off the constant human movement of personnel on shift. Through some quick thinking, social perceptiveness, and her ability to read people enough to formulate the perfect disguise, she got both her and Zoe inside the building by convincing others that they were lab assistants who had to monitor the specific flow shipments in and out of the depot area. Eventually, they got inside, where the real challenge started.

Once inside, Zoe told her it would be like facing a body's immune system. Every component of the building's security was set up to detect a breach and raise the alarm against invasive elements. Even though Zoe, by some miracle, managed to cause momentary glitches in the near-impenetrable system, it lasted long enough only to allow them the time to open and close the doors that would lead them to their quarry section by section. Quick escape would not be an option, so their entry had to be gradual enough to deflect any unwanted attention.

The particular level they found themselves on was home to the labs dedicated to computational biology, genetics, and a number of other branches that Indya couldn't even begin to fathom. The tenth floor. Each section was demarcated by a magnetic sliding door. Using her tablet, Zoe made short work of hacking into the security system long enough to blind the cameras and mute the alarms, which allowed her to plant one of her new toys. It was a depolarizer. Using an electrical surge, it changed the polarity of the magnets by which the door remained closed. This allowed the two-door panels to repel each other, pushing it wide open long enough for them to slip through.

After traipsing endlessly through clinical corridors and laboratories, they eventually reached their target: an opaque glass door engraved with DR. SEAN THOMPSON.

"We may have run into a bit of a problem," Indya commented.

"Why?" Zoe asked.

"His office door is not magnetic. It seems like the researchers included an additional layer of security in their offices. I noticed it a while back. It integrates biological markers. My... dad's office is pretty rudimental though, but more of a problem. It requires a retinal scan. How are we getting past that?"

"Well, luckily, I prepared for just such an eventuality. After his wife's comment on the similarities between you, I did a side by side comparison. I found a close enough match after doing an optical scan. We're going to need your eye."

"You established that from a photo?" Indya asked in disbelief.

"It's not an exact science, but close enough that I trust it." She dug in a pouch at her hip and withdrew a small device that looked like an infrared thermometer. Without warning, she placed her hand to the side of Indya's head to hold it still, leveling the machine right up to her eye for a few seconds before checking the display. Tapping it to make a few adjustments, she held it towards the retinal scanner. "Let's see if the overlay works. Your retinal scan should add more detail to the photograph of your father's eye. Thank God for HD cameras these days." The door's scanner beeped, and after what seemed like an eternity, the light glowed green, and the door opened.

They stepped into the office of Sean Thompson. If there was any doubt he was Indya's father, it faded as soon as she saw the old leather office chair he used to sit in at his college offices. A few of his favorite books lined some of the shelves. The rest of the space was alien to her. It was a fusion of a library and laboratory equipment that seemed to blend his two lives together. File cabinets lined the walls and were left unlocked so he could regularly access the files. Typical, she thought. For all the filing systems and security he invested in, he was still as disorganized as ever.

In the moments that Indya was taking in her father's blended lives, Zoe was already at his computer. "This is so odd. Your father has every single scrap of his research on his computer. Why would he have all the cabinets around?"

"He was devoted to what he was doing. He had backups for the backups, even if those backups were on paper. He was traditional that way."

"Well, I think I found all we need right here, so whenever he gets back, he will find his organized chaos untouched." She dug in her backpack and took out a hard drive.

"Really? You have magnetic depolarizers, software that can temporarily disable security systems, and gadgets to render any biomarker-protected entrance almost juvenile. Yet, you're going to make a ghost drive using that?" Indya almost laughed.

"Hey! Never underestimate old-school tech. Hard drives like this leave virtually no data traces that can track anyone back to us. It might take a while, though, which is why our timed entry into this place was so crucial. We want as little attention drawn to us as possible. The great thing about an ever-evolving digital age is that old tech becomes unpredictable as people forget about it. That includes security." Her fingers flew over the keyboard, and then she sat back in the chair to watch the monitor as the progress bar for the copied files was steadily filling.

Indya stared at the screen, almost trying to force the bar to load more quickly. Her eyes moved to the other one that stood blank next to it. "Hey, what's this for? It doesn't seem to be connected to the rest of the computer system."

Zoe looked. "Hmm. That... is a security monitor. See," she pointed, "the cable is tied down and snakes all the way to the floor and up the wall. I think it connects to a central server that casts security footage to its receivers."

"I think you need to fire that baby up, then. It might be

a good idea to have another eye on the hallways for anyone approaching. At the same time, we wait," Indya offered.

"Well, our breach was seamless. But you're the field girl, after all." Zoe started up the system. The monitor flashed to life to reveal a grid of nine images showing different views of the surrounding labs and hallways. "See nothing."

"Better safe than sorry."

Looking back at the computer monitor where the copying files were displayed, Zoe frowned. "O-K. This is odd."

"What is?"

"There is an icon here that started flashing in the tool-bar. It must have just appeared while I wasn't looking. Let me—" She stopped short then, her eyes growing wide as the color drained from her face. "Someone is watching this PC. It's remote security observation software."

"Dammit! So they're on to us."

"Not yet. I don't see anyone taking remote control of the system. If I was uploading this to a cloud, then they'd be all over my IP. Right now, they might just be browsing. They know the station is on, though, which is a problem." Zoe's eyes flew to the monitor. "Shit. We need to hurry. Luckily the files are almost copied. I see the guards moving up three levels down. And isn't that—"

"Jaydon! What the hell is he doing here?" Indya exclaimed. She answered her own question when she retrieved an earlier comment by her sidekick. "Elitelligence has the same automated system as this place. Of course."

"What?" Zoe said, sounding anxious.

"Never mind," Indya said, focusing her attention back on the live security footage.

"He is one level down, coming up fast. From the looks of it, he isn't going to take an elevator. I'm working on disabling those to buy us time." Amy had her tablet out, her fingers shaking ever so slightly as it flew over the touchpad.

Indya leaned over the security monitor, feeling a sweat breaking out over her forehead. "The stairway is the only exit from this level that connects down beside the elevators. If he is coming up that way."

"Then, we are trapped," Zoe finished.

ONCE ON THE HIGHWAY, Ariel pressed her foot down on the accelerator. She had a distinct feeling that something was wrong, and the shape of it had her sister's name written all over it. She was unsure whether it was the emotional turmoil of the last day or so that made her more attuned to her sister. Even though Indya hadn't emitted a psychic distress, Ariel had a powerful, intuitive drive that led her to the very edge of the inner city area.

As she took a secluded street down into the city proper, she drove through the business district. She reached an area where the architecture took on a more futuristic feel than some older buildings. The odd geometric corners and facades were as otherworldly as they were strangely beautiful. It divided this part of the city, and some of the older areas so much more distinct. Though the area primarily housed the bases of operations for medical centers and research councils, many financial service providers had found the appeal of the area irresistible as well. Eventually, it became a new hub of the urbanite movement and a coveted spot for property investors.

She passed the glistening exteriors of clinics and pharmaceutical companies, eventually turning a corner. She would have accelerated down the street had she not seen a familiar face: it was Jaydon. She was a little surprised. She thought it strange to find him in this part of the city but to be honest; she wasn't sure why the feeling was driving her toward this area either. Looking around, Ariel found a parking garage across the imposing crystalline shell of the building he stood in front of.

She climbed out of the car and walked up the steps to the landing right in front of the entrance. Noticing her, Jaydon turned around, surprised to see her. "Ariel? What are you doing here?"

She didn't know how to answer. "I was just driving in the area trying to find an address, but then I caught sight of you. So I thought—"

"Look," he started, almost dismissively, "now is really not a great time. I'm on the clock. Someone may have just broken into this place."

Ariel frowned, turning around to look at the large sign that dominated the archway adorning the entrance. It was BBS. Her heart skipped a beat for a moment as she put the pieces together. The psychic ping she was chasing felt stronger the longer she stood there and she had a good idea of who was inside—who Jaydon's culprit might be. Trying to compose herself, she didn't look around as she asked, "Did you catch them?"

"No," Jaydon answered, sounding frustrated. "I was sure we had them blocked off, but they threw up a couple of smokescreens to cover their getaway. They hacked the central operating system. Lights were flashing, and doors were slamming inside like it was some fucking haunted house."

"Thank god," Ariel whispered under her breath. *Indya, what have you gotten yourself into?*

Somehow, she had no doubt that it was her sister inside.

The foreboding synchronized too well with the event and the setting. This must have been the place where her father worked. Indya must have been snooping around inside to find out what life their father had led when he moved on.

"They're still inside, though. We just don't know where."

The news sent a chill down Ariel's spine. He was right. There was distinct psychic energy in the place that she could just barely single out, among others. It was moving fast, but it was still in the labyrinth of security that Jaydon had implemented. Her boyfriend had become a random variable in this case's complicated formula, but that was something that she would plot out soon enough. Right now, she needed to offer her sister a diversion.

"Have you tried the elevators?" she asked, turning to him.

"The what?"

"The elevators. Indya and I investigated a case a couple of years ago where kidnappers were cornered in a hotel. One of them managed to tamper with the elevator controls enough to disable the elevator from the inside. When the cops came to look for them, they completely discounted the elevator as an escape route because the outside control panel didn't work, and they had closed the doors. Meanwhile, they were right inside. In arm's reach. Law enforcement searched all the stairwells instead. It left a gap at just the right moment for them to get out and go the other way."

"The elevators didn't work at all"

"Exactly." Ariel smiled. "They, therefore, knew that it would be the last place you'd look."

"Fuck." Jaydon turned around and tried to lower his voice as he barked orders over his two-way radio.

Ariel looked back up at the building, trying to gauge

where her sister could be inside. Several minutes passed before she noticed a shift in the psychic signatures wading indoors. Something drew her to the side of the building. Turning to see whether Jaydon was looking, she walked to the corner, looking around. She could see a cargo bay area, left quiet as the personnel on duty were driven to the side for interrogation. It was very late, and she found it strange that people were still working in the area at this time while the building looked abandoned.

A heartbeat later, she saw two figures emerging behind a truck, out of sight of Jaydon's task team standing close by. The lights illuminated one of the figures' faces just enough to reveal the dark veil of her twin sister's hair. She also picked up enough of a reading to be sure her eyes weren't deceiving her. She did not recognize the other figure. They ducked out of sight, rounding the corner of the building just as Jaydon started to walk toward her.

Her distraction, however simple, afforded Indya and her companion an escape. They wouldn't have hidden in the elevator. It was a deception upon a deception. Indya would have been one step ahead. Still, the chase wasn't over.

"Hey," Jaydon said, "thanks for the tip-off. I didn't even con—"

Ariel simply raised her hand. "It's not a problem. Really. Look, I can see you're busy."

"I really need to get back, yes. We need—"

"Go right ahead. Let's have dinner sometime, ok?" She was perhaps coming across as unintentionally snippy, but she was eager to be right on her sister's heels.

Jaydon looked taken aback a bit but then offered a smile and nodded. "I'd really like that. I'll call you tomorrow." He waved and rushed back into the building.

As soon as he was out of sight, she practically bolted for

her car. She nearly broke her key in the ignition to bring it to life and sped out of her parking spot. She still felt the psychic trace of her sister. It was faint but strong enough for her to pick up on Indya's tail. She saw a car emerging from the other side of the building and knew immediately that she needed to pursue it. She switched her headlights to dim.

She was led out of the city proper and right into a suburban area. She expected them to move the other way, back home. Instead, they drove further out and eventually came upon a small neighborhood of houses that were probably owned by affluent families—old money.

She slammed hard on the brakes when they turned into the driveway of the most inconspicuous of the dwellings. There was nothing particularly eye-catching about it. In fact, had she been driving through the neighborhood any other day, she might have missed it if she had blinked. But perhaps, she thought that was the point. Hiding in plain sight.

Deciding that she needed more stealth, she turned into a side street where her car could be obscured by the looming houses on either side. Working quickly, she dashed across the lawns while keeping to the shadows. She reached the descending garage door just as it was about to close, ducked, and then rolled inside to land face-down just behind the getaway car bumper. She heard footsteps exiting the room. Jumping lightly to her feet, she tiptoed behind and followed the retreating voices as they made their way down a flight of stairs. A door slid shut behind her, and she cursed to herself for the risk she was taking. There's no turning back now.

So instead, she descended, going down until fluorescent light illuminated the end. It flooded her vision as she reached the landing, framing the two figures she had been following. They whipped around as they saw her, and she watched her sister's face curdle into a look of indignation that mirrored her own.

"Ariel? What the hell—"

"—am I doing here?" she finished. "I could ask you the very fucking same!"

SIX

V_{and}V

WILLS COLLIDE

Zoe Daniels felt like she had been tossed between fire and gasoline. The two sisters were locked in an explosive verbal tiff that resulted from far more than discovering the hidden lair. She suspected that there had been tension building between the two of them for quite some time. The reveal of hidden secrets was merely the catalyst.

"You're following me now?" Indya exclaimed.

"I told you that I could sense when something was off. What? Did you think you'd be able to hide this from me forever?" Ariel asked exasperated.

Indya had divulged many of the secrets that the twins shared to her sidekick. Among them, she had mentioned that they once shared twin telepathy that made them nearly inseparable when they were teens. However, they had grown apart through the years, and the psychic connection had waned with time. They still worked well together in their detective work, but the bond they had felt was all but broken.

At least, that was what Indya told herself. Watching her now, Zoe was sure she was questioning whether that fact was still true. Perhaps she had grown less sensitive to Ariel's psychic trace. Her sister, on the other hand, did not seem to share a similar affliction.

"Is this what you're doing most nights—breaking into big corporations?" Ariel was taking it all in: the spyware, technology, and stealth attire were displayed like some espionage exhibit in that subterranean space. Zoe was sure the effect was similar to walking into a pantry and finding a cache of drugs or walking into a bedroom to find a bondage play cave. Finding out your twin had a spy lair could probably do a number on you if you were a detective. "You're going rogue against law enforcement, do you realize that?"

"You cannot even begin to understand the complexities of crime that are woven into the urban landscape. I am merely trying to even out the odds."

"Vigilante justice is hardly altruistic. You should know that from all the work we have done," Ariel retorted. She noticed something in the corner of her eye and looked over at a black cat suit hanging in one of the display cabinets. "That looks nearly identical to the—" Her eyes went wide. "Jesus! It's you! You're the cat burglar who's been running rampant in the suburbs. The art thief. We've been tracking that case for months! We both have, and you've been taking the lead. Oh my god you've been covering your tracks the entire time!" Ariel's voice was rising to a dangerous pitch that threatened to crack the glass display cases surrounding them.

"Well," Zoe interrupted, "she has been returning historical pieces back to museums to enrich our society's cultural heritage. Seems like a good cause."

"Anything seems like a good cause if you can convince yourself that it is. Whatever way you spin it, it's still stealing!" Ariel rebutted.

"You have no right to barge in here and make flagrant accusations like that!" Indya fired back. "What about the interesting cases you have been taking on lately? Hmm? You've been concealing details of a few of them to go solo on the investigations. If I didn't know any better, I'd say that the reason you're standing here is that you knew more about our father's case than you've led on!"

Ariel was speechless under the force of her sister's onslaught.

Zoe was itching to access the ghost drive they had copied. She started creeping to the computer, allowing the sisters' heated exchange to continue, before Ariel stopped her. "Oh, no, no, no. Where do you think you're going? Who the hell are you anyway? Are you the delusional side-kick praising her misguided missions?"

Indya interjected. "Enough! Ariel, I want you to get out. We can talk about this—"

"Right now!" Ariel finished. "You have the perfect opportunity to play open cards with me right now!"

"Good," Zoe interceded from the side. "Then allow me to play the first hand on her behalf. Ladies, I give you the infamous Dr. Sean Thompson." With that, she pressed a button on the keyboard, and an entire digital portfolio sprang up on the largest monitor.

Whatever the sisters were going to say evaporated as the information was displayed in walls of text next to snapshots of the man.

"What what's all this?" Ariel said in an almost breathless whisper.

"If I were to take a wild guess, this looks exactly like a criminal case profile that a detective would compile," Zoe answered.

Indya walked closer. "That's weird. There is no information about his birthdate. Most of this only covers information from his involvement at the BBS. His work history states that he was hired by a pharmaceutical company, AlphaPharm, before that period. He worked his way up. His biographical info seems almost sparse. Would a case file not be more comprehensive?"

"That's only page one," Zoe said eagerly. She scrolled through the carousel of documents until she found articles from five years prior. "He attained notoriety fairly quickly after he started. Once he was assigned his own lab, he started making breakthroughs. That is when he was hand-picked by BBS."

"Go back one, please," Ariel asked, enthralled by the person that was worlds apart from the one they remembered. Zoe scrolled back one document. After reading, Ariel pointed out, "This is an article noting one of his achievements. However, it hardly mentions exactly what he did. It is nothing but a puff piece. The one next to it is nearly identical but seems longer. The words have been censored out. This side notation by the agent who compiled the profile seems to point to that fact."

Zoe moved through the rest of the documents. "There are side notations everywhere, and none of these points to any of his research. In fact, it was a pattern. Public information on his research was never available."

"There was tax documentation filed in between some of those reports. It was covered in red. Move back a bit"

Complying, Zoe paged through the information until she reached the documents in question. Her eyes scanned through the information, and it wasn't long before she picked up why the document was bathed in red ink. "Oh my god, these belong—"

"To another person," Ariel finished. The income was a

telltale sign to all three women. "If Sean Thompson was a top-notch researcher, then he would be earning far more than what these records indicate."

"This man was a janitor. The real Sean Thompson worked for the University of California in San Diego. His records end five years before dad's disappearance," Indya said. Zoe saw how Ariel looked at her sister, probably because it was the first time either of them had used a more personal way of referring to their father.

"Dad was a college professor there," Ariel added.

"Yeah, no shit, Sherlock," Indya bit back. "We know. It obviously wasn't a coincidence."

"Listen, don't start with me. You're lucky I'm handling this a lot more coolly than you probably deserve. You have no right to be a bitch right now." Ariel had made a switch reasonably quickly, Zoe had to admit. She was visibly controlling her temper, though. Indya looked about ready to react with another snarky comment, but Zoe decided to cut her off.

"Before you too get too spicy again, let's focus on the facts here. Your father died ten years ago. Sean Thompson, the scientist, didn't exist until a week after that. Sean, the janitor, died five years before the scientist was reborn. They worked in the same institution, close enough that your dad would have known about his passing. It was the perfect disguise. He could assume an identity that became vacant. So he did. He stole it, and in fact, repurposed it. No one really cares about who Sean Thompson was before he was an acclaimed researcher. But those details still fill the uninvestigated vacuum of years before your father's notoriety. As for the five years, no one would really care enough to look into where he disappeared to. Someone could easily get rid of a death certificate or erase documentation that denies that Sean Thompson actually died. For five years, instead of being dead, he was 'alive.' Long enough for your father to possibly work out the kinks until he was comfortable to step into the persona publicly."

The twins just stared at her. For people that looked so similar, they couldn't be more different. Ariel's face was scrunched in a calculated display of marvel. Indya's face carried a distinct 'what the fuck' bafflement to it. There was an awkward silence as Zoe's surmise of the scenario set in before she broke the silence again. "It would appear, ladies, that your father could teach you a thing or two about being covert."

"I don't even know where to go from here. If this is a case profile on himself, then why would he have it? We were the first to take the case." Ariel asked.

"Not exactly," Indya offered. "His wife mentioned that there had been others who had investigated, but none of them could unearth a whole lot about him. Others simply never came back to her at all. She tried establishing contact, but she could never find them. She even had detectives looking for other agents who were on the case."

Ariel was fuming, and between gritted teeth, she said, "You knew about that and just casually forgot to mention that detectives have been disappearing on the case?"

Indya answered coolly, "I didn't think it was—"

"Important?" Ariel finished. "Do you see what I'm seeing? An entire case docket existed with information that we would have only found after months—if you didn't go against the books in any case. Whatever he was up to, it was damn important enough that he made sure he had it so no authority could get their hands on it."

Indya wanted to retort, but her sister's point got her to

thinking. "So if he has his own case file, then what happened to the agent?"

"Nothing good," Zoe commented from the side. While the sisters were arguing, she had been digging through the rest of the ghost drive. It finally revealed what the twin's father had been working on. "At least, that is my suspicion. Your father wasn't just any kind of bioengineer. Whatever he had been busy with, he had carried over research he had started years ago in his days as a professor. Finally, he found the means to execute the first test when he was given a laboratory. He took it to the next step." Zoe clicked around the screen, adjusting the setting to project a new image on the monitor in front of them.

She didn't know who gasped first, but Ariel was the first to say something in response to the anatomical diagrams and accompanying photos that met their eyes. "He was trying to create super humans."

SEVEN

V_{and}V

DECEIT RUNS THICKER THAN BLOOD

The next morning, Ariel headed out early. Despite their insistence that she might as well stay over because of the hour, Ariel wanted to sleep in her own bed. Things between her and Indya were complicated. Her mind was reeling from the deceptions and secrets. Ariel needed to process things and really sleep on them. She wouldn't be able to do that on a stranger's couch.

Sleep had come, if sporadically, but it wasn't long before Ariel decided that she was fed up with trying to get any rest. She knew of at least one person who would be awake by now, and she was convinced that he might have a few answers.

Uncle Ted lived in a modest house on the edge of her neighborhood. The man had practically raised them after their parents' now alleged passing. After college and the pursuit of their careers, Ariel thought to find a place that was still close enough to check in every now and then. He was more than surprised to see her knocking at his door.

He led her to his study, which looked more like a library than anything else. Couches replaced the desk that would ideally have been standing in the middle. There were far too many books for the shelves to contain. So instead, the excess volumes were stacked in haphazard piles on the floor. Some might have thought of it as disorganized, but Ariel saw it as a sanctum of knowledge.

Her uncle returned with two cups of coffee. It was already his second, but he always enjoyed a couple throughout the day. "I haven't seen you in a while, and never this early on a Sunday. Something tells me this is not a random check-in."

"No. Look, Uncle, I can mince around with words, but I'm too frazzled by something to make small talk. I need you to tell me about the type of work my father got into while he was working as a professor."

Her uncle nearly spilled his coffee as he placed his mug on the coffee table, distracted by the subject she had raised. "Your father? Well, he was involved in bioengineering"

"Yes, I know," she interrupted, maybe too harshly, "but that is a vast field in its own right. He didn't work with things like ecological engineering or the design of medical equipment. He was interested in genetics. In fact, I have done some digging and come to believe that he was almost fanatical about it."

Ariel could see he was tentative as he carefully weighed his response. After a while, he cleared his throat to answer. "Well, he was devoted. You are right. He was interested in the modification and augmentation of biological systems so that they could function and maintain themselves better. He sometimes did pro bono research to aid projects run by pharmaceutical agencies that were testing new ranges to their medicines."

"So he was altering DNA," Ariel stated.

"That is a very rudimental summary of it, but in a way, yes."

Ariel leaned forward before asking. "How long had he entertained the idea of breeding superhuman traits?"

"W-what do you mean?" he asked, unsure of the sudden turn in severity laced within her tone.

"Did he ever talk of super humans and magnificent traits that can be bestowed on people with the right genetic altering?"

"Ariel, I don't know where—"

"You know what Indya and I can do, don't you?"

He wasn't ready for an interrogation. Perhaps it was unfair that she was subjecting him to one, but she wanted answers. "What is this all about, Ariel?"

"I want to know whether me and my sister became some morbid fascination for him in terms of our abilities. I want to know whether we were the result of some of his experiments."

Her uncle looked long and hard at her. "You think your sister and yourself are bioengineered."

"Yes. It's the only thing that can explain one of the mysteries we could never solve, despite using its consequences to our advantage. We both can read minds. Indya has the ability to heal quickly, which means that she is constantly operating at 150 percent. And my kinesthetic abilities have been greatly enhanced. It is all I can do to just try to physically slow down from time to time."

He folded his hands in a contemplative gesture as he looked at her. "I can see this has become really overwhelming for you. But Ariel, some of your ideas are beginning to border on the insane."

She groaned. Fed up with all the deflections of the truth she was being presented with. "I just wish someone would tell me the whole goddamn truth." Standing up, she started to pace around the room.

"Come on, Ariel, sit down. Join me for breakfast, and then we can talk about what you've been going through. We can—Ariel?"

She wasn't listening. As her eyes had moved across the shelves, she noticed a book that didn't quite match the series among which it was placed. Though her uncle had a broad collection of scientific textbooks and journals in his possession, they all occupied the shelves to the right. On the left, he collected classic literature and fiction. Of the books in the case, at least one shelf was entirely stacked with children's folktales, which he used to read when they were very young. Yet, in the middle stood one book that did not match —a summary of modern genetics. Unlike the hardcover books to either side, its paperback binding stood out from the faded tomes surrounding it. Almost organically, Ariel walked closer, reaching out.

Her uncle, perplexed, watched her for a while to figure out what she was doing, but as he deduced her aim, he nearly fell out of his seat as he tried to stop her.

It was too late. Ariel slid the book from the shelf. The particular case immediately shifted and opened outward, revealing a small cubicle just large enough to fit a desk. A single light switched on at the top and revealed inner shelves surrounding the niches, stacked with bound documents and notes. The draft that drifted in as the case swung open blew papers from the small desk to land right at Ariel's feet. She didn't have to look long to recognize her father's handwriting.

"Am I just being crazy again," she started, picking up the notes, "or are my eyes the only thing not feeding me deceptions?"

Her uncle was speechless. She could see that he was desperately scrambling in his mind for a response, but she had learned long ago that guilt is the one thing that writes itself most clearly on someone's face.

As he was staring at the irrefutable evidence that she held in her hand, he swallowed hard before closing his eyes in preparation for revealing the truth. "You are not crazy. What you are holding is indeed his research. And the two of you were his only breakthroughs."

Ariel reeled at the news but made sure that it didn't show on her face. "Uncle Ted please tell me what is going on."

"Ariel, the first thing you need to know is that I am not your uncle. I was your father's lab assistant, years ago. Before I continue, I really think you should sit—"

"Don't try to calm me down!" she responded, pacing herself in her rising anger and confusion. "Just tell me the goddamn truth!"

He raised his hand in defense. "Alright, alright." He took a deep breath before continuing. "Your father started to experiment with modifications on the human genome. His goal was not to change the genetic code but find a way to enhance what was already there. What he proposed seemed almost mad at the start—the cultivation of super abilities. But I thought, idealistic as I was that his vision was revolutionary. When he was finally successful, I could not help but devote my efforts to his dream."

"What did he do?" Ariel asked, her voice level but her hands quivering. "What was his success?"

He looked her right in the eye as he answered. "You, you, and your sister." He sighed, as though reminiscing, and then continued. "There were others, subjects that displayed the enhanced abilities he was cultivating, but their own fates ended badly. They went mad, as if not only their bodies but even their minds were rejecting the 'improvements.' Few—none—made it, save for the two of you."

"So we were nothing but his lab rats. It sounds like he wasn't even our father." Her uncle gave her a blank stare in answer, confirming her suspicion. "What about our mother? Are we her children, or was that an additional fabrication?"

"The woman you remember was your mother by birth. That was never a lie. Her attachments to you complicated long-term research. She would never let you go for the sake of science. Your 'father' was not prepared to let go of his creations either. So, he married her and went against our protocols to include her and the two of you in his life. That way, he could monitor how your genotypes would manifest over the years."

This time, Ariel did sit down. The revelations just never slowed. In a single weekend, her world had imploded, and she was questioning everything about the way her life had assumed its current shape. "Are you working with him now?"

"What?"

"I said, are you working for him now?" Ariel was investing a serious effort to bite back her anger.

"Ariel, I don't understand. Your father is dead. He has been for many years. Both your parents are."

She knitted her brow in confusion. "Gavin—my supposed father—has been posing as a man called Sean Thompson for nearly ten years. He worked as a bioengineer for the Bureau of Biogenics Sciences in their branch here in Fleetwood City. He remarried, and his wife only recently opened a case file with our agency to track him down. He never stopped his work. We found years of research and tests were done that prove it. He has had the alibi, the support, and the resources."

Ted's eyes went wide. "No. No, this cannot be. He can't be alive. We've sacrificed too much to keep you safe."

Ariel was dumbstruck. The last thing she expected to hear was any semblance of news that was indicative of danger. "What are you saying?"

"Ariel, if your father is alive if he went missing then it means someone was after him and his research. Most of his archived studies will undoubtedly make mention of you, even if you both were part of the genesis of the career path he chose. There are people, dangerous people, whose attention he attracted over the years. Trust me when I tell you if they ever pick up the trail on either one of you and tie you back to his work, they'll be very intrigued with the idea of acquiring you as their own experiments."

ON THE ONE HAND, Indya was less than eager to return home. Still, she felt exhausted. The confrontation with Ariel was both unforeseen and draining. She had utterly misjudged her sister and had almost become too complacent as a result. Even though their twin telepathy had waned because of their fractured bond, it didn't negate the intuitive feelings that still connected them. Nor did it take away Ariel's other abilities.

She wished she had been more careful. She should have had a contingency in place for when her sister became suspicious. Ariel was like a bloodhound, always finding her quarry. She could track nearly anyone but also had the ability to chase them down. Indya forgot just how fast her sister moved if she was driven enough. It was a dangerous power to be up against when your only option was to run.

By that reasoning, the Den was located under Zoe's place, just one suburb over. It was close enough to access in a pinch but far enough to not draw attention.

Indya arrived at their shared home, parked, and headed in. She took a deep breath before opening the door, only to find that it was locked. She frowned, as she had been ready to find Ariel at home. The house stood empty. The telltale signs like untouched coffee, ruffled sheets and a pile of clothes from the previous evening were evidence enough that her sister had been there. Maybe she had left early in the morning. This time, it was Indya who felt apprehensive.

Whatever remnant of telepathy was left to her had been reactivated, and she immediately had the feeling that something was wrong. After such a long time, the sensation was odd as it washed over her, yet all too familiar. Regardless of the tension that may have existed between them, she needed to go out and find her sister—wherever she was.

Just as she was about to head out, there was a knock on the door. "Who would be—" Looking at her watch, she noticed that it was after 9. It wasn't that early, but a visitor at this time on a Sunday was a little unorthodox. She walked back to the foyer, reached the front door, and opened it to find Jaydon.

Every fiber of her being tensed as she saw him standing there. There was enough reason for her to feel that level of discomfort. It had been twice now that she had barely escaped a run-in with him while doing some off-the-record espionage. The last had nearly resulted in them being caught. They had been lucky, thanks to some quick thinking on Zoe's part.

Despite that, he was unpredictable. His mental blocks

rendered her ability useless at reading his mind. She realized just how much she relied on it to navigate the people she came across.

"Good morning," he said cheerfully.

"Why are you here?" Her response was a bit hostile. She knew she needed to be careful. Otherwise, she unlocks suspicion.

"Damn, it seems like you've had quite the night. I thought I'd drop in to check on your sister. I had a late night with some emergency, and kind of had to cut it short when she happened to drive past the scene I was investigating last night."

Indya had nearly forgotten the fact that her sister was at the institute. She wondered if Ariel had anything to do with helping in their escape. She was almost sure she did. "She isn't here, Jaydon. I think it's better you come back tomorrow."

"I'm set to see her tonight anyway. Frankly, I didn't think it really mattered when we checked in with each other. I just really want to see her."

He started to irritate her then. "God, you've seen her nearly every day in the last week alone. Can't you take a break? One might start to think you're getting a bit clingy." Her rudeness was deliberate, but a part of it felt genuine.

The friendliness slowly melted from his face, steadily being replaced by a look of scorn at her hostility. "Relationships develop with effort and investment, not by convenience. We're both busy people, Indya. If we don't take the time to see each other as much as we can, then that lack of commitment will spell the end of us. I love your sister. I'd like for this to work."

"You've been dating for less than a year, my friend," she challenged him. "Let's not get too excited. I've watched the dynamic between you, and to be honest, I don't really think you're nearly as serious as you let on." She leaned closer, bringing her voice down to a menacing whisper. "I don't trust you. For that reason, I don't really like you. I don't know what your intentions are, but I doubt they match up as well to your confessions as you're making everyone believe. Whatever they are, I want you to keep them far away from my sister. And if you plan something know that I'll be watching."

The stare-off that ensued was lethal. Neither of them was less formidable than the other. They were counterparts in their willpower. Indya was sure that he knew as well as she did that neither of them was about to reveal more than the stony expressions that measured the other coolly in the space that separated them.

After a while, Jaydon merely smirked, nodded, and walked away. As he turned, he said, "Tell your sister I came around and to give me a call if you want. You'll be seeing me soon enough either way." It left her cold, but she shook it off and closed the door. She would wait a time after he left, and then she'd do the same. She needed to find her sister. A sense of foreboding filled her. She could just feel that things were about to assume a different pace.

AFTER DRIVING AROUND for nearly an hour, Indya was about to give up and head home to wait for Ariel there. She had tried following the twin pull with mixed success—feeling as if she lost the trail as soon as she was hot on it. However, just as she was about to give up, she felt drawn down a street that curved close to the river. Sure enough, as she was driving, she saw a lone figure sitting on a bench overlooking the water.

Making her own parking spot upon a dirt patch just off the roadside, Indya got out and jogged toward where Ariel was sitting. Her sister looked like she was in a state. It was clear she hadn't slept the night before, and she would not have been surprised if her morning had started roughly too.

She didn't announce herself as she arrived. She was sure Ariel had sensed her coming miles away. So Indya simply sat down next to her and looked out over the river where the sun caught the water in motion. They remained that way, silent for quite some time. Neither of them spoke, but there was a psychic exchange of emotional impressions that neither could vocalize, yet both understood.

Ariel was eventually the first to speak. "It's funny how quickly things change once you set off a chain reaction. We should be used to it, I guess, being detectives and all. There is never a mild truth hidden behind a lie. More often than not, you find that the truth cascades out once the fabric of the lie is torn."

It was a powerful statement, and Indya simply soaked in those words before asking, "So, what changed?"

"Everything. It changed, simply because an illusion cannot hide reality forever." She looked at her sister with red, tired eyes. "They lied to us, Indya about everything."

"Start at the beginning," Indya gently coaxed, placing her hand over her sister's. Ariel did, and as more of the story was unfurled, she wished it had stopped at the beginning. Her sister filled in the gaps about their father, about his work, and about them. She spoke of Uncle Ted and how the fabrications were far deeper than any of them could have imagined. She even alluded to the danger and how the recent turn of events might have created a peril that neither saw coming.

When her sister had told her everything, Indya wasn't exactly sure how she was supposed to feel. In part, she found it amusing that it took her sister one familial visit to find out all she had. It took her and Zoe an entire expertly synchronized secretive operation to uncover mere pieces of a larger puzzle. She also felt a sense of trepidation. Neither of them had mentally prepared themselves to be caught in a narrative that had already started years ago. When they believed in a life, that was their only reality.

"Please tell me what's on your mind," Ariel nudged her sister.

"It would be easier to tell you what isn't. You know, we should really fall into a habit again of utilizing our psychic bond."

Ariel managed a smile. "Yeah, we probably should."

Indya leaned forward, resting her elbows on her knees. She looked down at her feet for a moment and then gave Ariel a taunting smile. "You know, not to be the one to say I told you so but you do know that this means that both our parents are likely alive."

Ariel pursed her lips, staring back out across the river before answering. "I know. I'm just not sure how I feel about finding them. Or them finding us."

EIGHT

CHESS PIECES

The sisters woke up the next morning in a haze. Their weekend had amounted to far more than either of them could have ever wished upon themselves. The coffee pot boiled more than once as they attempted to become more human. They downed two mugs, whipped up breakfast from whatever was left in the house, and steadily made to their leave. Though they both felt foggy, Ariel did notice an energy shift. Something had cleared between the two of them, and though they had yet to fully regain their twin connection, she did feel more attuned to her sister than ever before.

Consequently, it didn't escape her that there was something on Indya's mind as if she was working up to tell her something. Yet, Ariel didn't feel like forcing the issue. She decided to allow Indya to open the conversation. As the morning progressed and they finally felt ready to take on the day, her sister did just that as they climbed in her car.

"Ariel, I want to talk about Jaydon."

Ariel wasn't sure if she expected any mention of him but nonetheless conceded. "Ok. What's up?"

"Obviously, you know he was running the security operation at the BBS headquarters. Now, to me, that already arouses suspicion, but it wasn't the only time I've had an encounter with him."

"You're referring to your quote-unquote 'other' obligation?"

"Yeah. I managed to evade him on Friday night as well. I didn't know he was involved with Elitelligence. Zoe came across them at some stage when one of our leads led through their halls. Inadvertently, she picked up that their servers were all but unhackable. From what we could gather, his security team was tasked to safeguard research firms dealing with data processing and analysis by outsourcing researchers to larger companies. For a niche research agency, that kind of security seemed worth investigating. Anyway, as I was planting a device that would allow us access from the inside, Jaydon showed up."

Ariel raised an eyebrow. "Sounds like you were the one to cut my date short."

"Yeah, well, your boyfriend was too busy with some shady business to stay—in my opinion."

"You were the one breaking in, and he is the one being shady?" Ariel laughed. "You do know what that sounds like, don't you?"

"Yeah, yeah. Whatever. You're missing the point. I am starting to believe that BBS may have made use of these research agencies to manage and store their projects' data in their vaults. These locations were full of additional labs that seemed to be in operation. It is possible that BBS moved their more risky experiments off-site, to a place that didn't attract as much attention, but where the security was none-theless as airtight. After you left, Zoe uncovered some documents from both facilities that indicate that they have been linked in multiple projects. Jaydon's security company is involved in protecting them. That leads me to believe that somehow, he could well be a part of all this."

They arrived at work, and Ariel parked the car as she was talking, "We're talking about the entire institute here, though. Not all of the experiments and projects are tied to Dad." Referring to Sean Thompson as their father was still strange, to say the least. Ariel had a frog in her throat more than once, using the term of endearment so loosely.

"Don't worry," Indya said, probably reading her thoughts, "I find it odd to think of him that way as well." They climbed out and headed into the office before she continued. "Look, all I am suggesting is to be careful. We've learned that there are a couple of people we have trusted that were not forthcoming. We need to be careful of who we open ourselves to regarding our lives." With that, Indya turned and headed to her office, effectively ending the conversation.

When Ariel sat down behind her own desk, she was more than ready to discard Indya's suspicions, but she couldn't shake the truth of her sister's last words. The fact that Jaydon was contracted to secure the places Indya had snuck into could just be a coincidence. Still, she couldn't understand why he didn't question the tight security that BBS required. From what Indya had nudged at, it seemed to be far more intense than the normal protection services he had told them he offered.

Mulling over it, she picked up her phone to call him. She couldn't wait around for dinner. She wanted to get to the bottom of this sooner.

AT LUNCHTIME, she waited at The Olive Pit, purposefully arriving earlier to get her mind straight. She couldn't rely on her ability to scope out the truth, so her line of questioning needed to be well thought out. She still felt her heart palpitate wildly as he walked in. She felt ridiculous. He shouldn't be able to unsettle her. Yet, after all that had happened, caution was turning everyone into an enemy in her eyes.

When he saw her, he smiled. Walking around the table, he kissed her on the cheek and then sat down. "God am I happy you chose this place. Good thinking about moving our date to lunch. I'm starving. I would have probably skipped lunch again to my own detriment."

"Really? Are you guys that busy?"

He nodded. "The new contracts have a hefty set of stipulations by which they want us to enforce security."

"You mean like the place I found you at?" she asked, trying to keep her tone neutral.

"Yeah. Them and some other corporations."

"So," she started her mind racing between keeping her composure and carefully weighing her words. "I don't think I've ever asked this, but how does your security company operate?" He cocked his head to the side, almost bemused by her question. "You've never been interested in that before."

"Yeah, I know," she answered, feeling as though her heart could jump out of her chest. "I was just curious if that type of security was the only thing you guys specialized in. I don't know, I was maybe wondering if you, um, did fieldwork as well." She didn't feel as if she was approaching it as smoothly as she thought.

His eyes sparkled up, and somehow she knew she had unknowingly ventured into the right line of questioning.

"Oh, I get it! The other day I mentioned I could potentially help you on a case. Networking and tracking and all that. That must be why you're asking!"

To be honest, she had forgotten he even offered. But she was more than willing to accept an excuse that he so openly provided. "Um yeah. You got me."

"Are you folks ready to order?" It was the waitress.

"Two of your meals of the day, please! I caught the aromas of flatbread just as I walked in. My mouth was watering," Jaydon said.

"Sure thing," the waitress said, scribbling a short note. "It should be ready in about ten minutes or so." She took the menus and left.

"So, where were we? Oh yeah. Basically, Elitelligence began as a small company offering standard security to small businesses and retailers. We didn't really work in the city as much as we worked on its edges, catering to these indie brands and startups. We've managed well in instituting high-tech systems that could match the high-tech ecology of the places we offered our services. Everything is moving online, so digital security became as important as physical barriers. It was something that was actually perfectly suited to the needs of bigger clients."

"Like pharmaceutical companies and clinical research institutes? I'm just guessing."

"You're exactly on the mark. It was actually something my father realized when he started the company. When he stepped down, I didn't venture into it immediately. They found us, and then business was really booming."

They more than likely didn't have the capital to afford it without some significant investment, she suspected. "So, besides high-tech security solutions, what else drew their attention to you?"

"Track-and-trace maneuvers," he answered, smiling.

She felt herself go cold. "What?"

"Our security systems were not only designed to enable us to stop intruders in their tracks but to enable us to track them once they intrude. It is not a perfect system yet, but we've had some success. We can retrace the interference with our security systems from the moment they were hacked, such as where the signals emanated from or at which points they were received. That way, we almost draw a path by which burglars moved once they got inside. It gives us hotspots of physical interaction that may help us find DNA samples, for instance, fingerprints left on door frames or even hair follicles that may have fallen off. You know, one thing that security often does is simply look at the epicenter of the crime scene, such as the computer that was hacked or the room broke into. They never try to retrace the route of the culprits, which can be a goldmine of evidence. It is often on the way in, and the way out, where people slip up."

Damn it, Indya, Ariel thought, he may be on to you yet. She hoped her sister was as good as the media had salaciously painted her in the art robberies' coverage.

"That brings me back to how we could help you. Perhaps—"

"Jaydon, stop. I haven't been completely honest with you. I think I've been stalling for time by talking about all this." God, Ariel, I hope you're making the right judgment call here, she told herself.

He was confused. The excitement that was written over his features disappeared in an instant. "There's something else on your mind then?"

"I—God, this is such a cliché, but I think we need to take a break."

She may as well have torn his heart out. His face was a confusing mix of emotions as he processed what she proposed. "Is this about the other night? Ariel, if I moved too quickly by telling you how I felt about you, I'm sorry. I can take a step back, move at your pace."

She held up her hand to stop him. Forced apathy gave her a strange control over a situation when she felt she didn't have any. "Look, J, I just I need time. Lately, things have really thrown me a curveball. I'm just not comfortable exposing you to this side of me. I really just need time."

He looked as though he had a million things he wanted to say, but none of them were making it past his lips. So instead, he said the most chivalrous thing any man could say in the throes of his tumultuous feelings. "Alright," he answered solemnly, "take all the time you need. I'll wait."

"I have to go." Looking at him, she wished she had it in her to offer him some consolation, but she simply stood up and gave him a gentle squeeze on the shoulder before she left. Detached as it was, she could not deny the relief that washed over her as she stepped out of the restaurant. The facts were that her father's case was making divided attention difficult, and she had little to offer for a relationship.

Yet, it was not the determining factor.

Jaydon, whether intentionally or not, had become dangerous. If he managed to get close to Indya's trail, Ariel would be the perfect mediator to confirm his suspicions. She knew what her sister had done, and she was sure he would find a way to expose it if he was on to them. The way he had boasted about Elitelligence's methods gave her pause. It was done with relentless zeal. If she and her sister were to get deeper into this case, then he would be more hell-bent on picking up their trail. The fact that they couldn't read him proved problematic. If he ever suspected them, she would not be sure whether he was ever lying to her—perhaps to try and coax them into a trap.

Right now, he could not be trusted, and it broke her heart to admit it to herself. The tears came of their own accord, making her walk away even faster.

"YOU KNOW, just because you called this place, The Storm Den doesn't mean that it needs to look like it belongs to an animal. This place is a wild mess!" Indya exclaimed, walking into the spy lair, which had become something akin to an art installation composed of sticky notes, string, hanging photos, and documents plastered all over the walls.

"Listen bitch, I am nothing if not thorough," Zoe retorted. "Besides, you have never dealt with a case quite as complex as this. This is all just absolutely insane!"

"Good, I'm going to need as much dirt as you can give me. Did you get my messages?"

"On the skeletons that were ripped out of your family's closet? Yeah! Geez, how are you feeling? Sorry, I realize I hardly ever ask. Once you get into these investigations."

"It becomes addictive, and you lose track of everything else," Indya finished with a smirk. "I know."

"So how does it feel being a breakthrough in modern science?" Zoe asked teasingly. Some of us had to slack behind in the evolutionary gene pool, you know, and we didn't turn out all that impressive. Meanwhile, you two kids are way ahead of us all!"

"Nobody gave the man a Nobel Prize yet. Let's not think too much of ourselves here. In all seriousness, though, this whole thing is taking on a different pace by the day. I want to know if my father faked his own death on purpose.

Was it a strategic play on his part? Was he forced to make that decision and assume a new life? We need to start separating reality from mystery here. I want to know how much of our memories were not part of some illusion."

"Well, I started digging the minute you messaged, but I couldn't find anything relating directly back to those facts. When it comes to personal history, your dad wasn't big on journaling. As for being a reflexive note-taker in his role as a scientist, well, that is a different story." She walked over to the back of one counter and lifted a pin-up board that she set on the surface.

"All these screens, and you still use those?" Indya asked.

"To see the entire picture, you sometimes need good old, faithful methods. Now, check this out. These are brain imaging scans that I found under the field notes of a folder labeled Project Alpha."

"The oldest ones dated back twenty five years ago. And the most recent ones are from this year."

"Correct, and look right below them."

"These are the actual field notes. At least a much reduced version of them. But it's odd; some of those relating to older experiments look newly written compared to some of the more recent ones."

"You haven't lost your touch, after all," Zoe said, winking. "Your father only started the practice of note-taking a year after his alleged death. Those are the start of the handwritten notes you see there. About five years into his life as Sean Thompson, he started digital documentation. He continued that practice till the very end."

"But the notes about the earliest dates of research look similar to the latest. He jotted down the information using the same methods and mnemonics by which to label the particular experiment. In comparison, the start of the handwritten notes looks almost haphazard, with no system of organization at all. It was almost as if he had lost his earliest work."

Zoe smiled. "That was one of the first red flags I picked up as well. Also, notice how sparse the information on some of those earlier notes is. So many gaps compared to the others. That was another indicator. I think he was trying to remember facts but couldn't quite recall it all."

Indya must have looked pensive as she stared hard at each clue. "And these scans I dread to say it, but these are test subjects, aren't they?"

"Yep. Electroencephalography and Positron Emission Tomography. The first set illustrates the brain under certain psychological conditions, while the second shows where the neurons are firing. In conjunction with the notes, they point to another interesting fact."

Indya followed the research timeline for a moment, looking at the scans and reading the reflections on the experimental subjects below. After a while, she noticed the pattern Zoe was alluding to. "His success rate was declining. The brain scans show reduced activity as the years go on. Some of the post-experimental results show no difference from normal states. This research peaked early, and then he could never duplicate the success. It's like he was retracing his steps."

"I think so too," Zoe agreed. "You wanted answers to why he switched lives, but I cannot give you a clear answer there. What I can tell you is this: there was a clear interruption between when he 'died' and when he resumed research, and it really impacted his entire methodology. I am tempted to think that it was because of this research that his decisions led him to where it did."

Indya shook her head, walking away from the board as

she tried to mull through her father's reasoning. "Something doesn't add up. His career skyrocketed as Sean Thompson, eventually attracting attention from the BBS. You saw the office we snuck into. The man was well-funded and generously resourced. He had all the means to come close to recreating his success. Are you telling me his rudimentary backyard experiments as a college professor yielded more success than his time as an acclaimed scientist?"

"If he lost his initial research, then yes. I went through the drive. Detailed accounts and research reports only exist for the last ten years. Everything that should have preceded that are just recreated accounts that don't quite do the results justice. Especially here." She was pointing to the board at two sections of brain imaging scans that displayed high activity. It was taken at the very beginning of his success streak. Rereading the notes, Indya couldn't help but pick up how the scientific reflections almost became sentimental. "Is this...?"

"You and your sister? I think so. You were a success story he could rewrite."

Indya's phone suddenly started ringing. She dug in her back pocket and answered. "Hello. Ariel... what...? Alright, hang on, I'm opening the door. I, um, guess you know the way down now." She hung up, and then walked to a wall panel that accessed the security system. "It's Ariel. She's in front of the garage."

"Um, how has she taken the whole discovery of this place?" Zoe asked, shifting uncomfortably as she waited for the dynamic of the room to change.

"With a past of being a bioengineered superhuman and a duplicitous father that basically became her Frankenstein, I think the discovery of a secret vigilante base was horribly overshadowed."

At the next moment, the door opened, and Ariel stepped into the Den. It was clear she had been crying. Indya knew something had happened in the time since they'd seen each other this morning. "God El, what's wrong? Please tell me you didn't discover more crazy shit about—"

"I just broke up with Jaydon," she stated bluntly, in an almost hollow voice.

Indya was speechless but not particularly upset. "Oh. Um... That happened quickly. What brought you to that decision?" She didn't know how to get soppy or be an emotional buffer, mostly if she felt the turn of events necessary.

Ariel took a deep breath, looked them both in the eyes, and answered. "Strategy. I think I've been sidetracked by confusion at the start of all this. Right now, I need my head in the game. Besides I think you're right. Jaydon is an external variable at this point that could upset our recovery of the truth. His company is entrenched in this whole saga. They may be neutral, but I don't know how long it will be before picking a side. If he finds out what we're trying to do, I don't know whether he's with us. That's enough reason for me to put some distance between us."

Indya had her arms crossed as she listened. She simply nodded before responding. "I think you made the right decision. I'd love to hear the details later."

"I am going to agree with her," Zoe put in from the side.

The sisters looked her way and saw how she already doing her own thing behind a computer. Indya smiled to herself. Trust Zoe to be efficient, even amid a serious moment. She wasn't salacious at all. She kept her nose out of people's private business.

"If he is their guard dog, then it's a good thing you upset

him enough to be distracted—no offense, of course. I don't know how I overlooked this, but there was a location tag on some of these photos. I punched in the coordinates, and it leads to a facility just out of town. I suspect it may be where he conducted most of these experiments. Or at least, where some of them may have been kept."

Ariel frowned. "He had an entire facility to use at BBS, though. Why would he experiment off-site?"

Zoe took a deep breath before looking her straight in the eye. "Oh honey, with the types of crap your father got into, he would be breaching every damn ethical code they had! If I was him, I would have hidden the evidence in the Nevada desert."

Indya walked over to stand beside Zoe. As she scrupulously scanned what her assistant had open on the computer screen, her own eyes widened. She looked at Indya feeling a mixture of shock, melancholy, and stern resolve. "It's time we went on a monster hunt."

NINE

V~and~V

WOLF'S DEN

"Ariel. Hey, ARIEL!"

She snapped out of it and looked over at Indya. "What? What is it?"

"Did you hear me?" her sister asked. "Did you process anything I just said?"

"You said something?" Ariel asked innocently. She had been staring out the passenger's window of the car. They were en route to the location Zoe discovered among Sean's notes.

"O-K. Taking that as a hard 'no.' I was asking if you're ready."

"Um," Ariel didn't know how to answer if she had to be honest with herself. In three days, her entire world felt like it had fallen apart. She wished she had her sister's thick skin when it came to emotional hassles. She was more rational but also more prone to shut down in the face of adversity. The hesitation was all the sign her sister needed.

"Taking that as a negatory as well. Look, sis, I can sense you're a bit off your rocker here, but it's like you're thinking out loud without intending to. I'm taking a wild guess that our twin telepathy is gaining its mojo back. Comforting as that is, I can sense you're distracted. That kind of puts me on edge. With these types of missions, I'm pretty focused. Distractions lead to mistakes, and mistakes leave a trail for others to pick up. Suppose everything you said about Jaydon's operation is true. In that case, we need to execute this with near surgical perfection, or else he'll be onto us."

"I know, Indya, I know," Ariel answered, feeling overwhelmed. "Look, I'll try to get my head in the game."

Her sister couldn't look at her long enough to gauge whether she was serious. She had to keep her eyes on the road. Perhaps it was for the best. She was sure her mind was scrambled enough to send all kinds of confusing telepathic red flags Indya's way. It was better than her expression didn't give anything away. Indya simply nodded, tensing her jaw as she accepted her sister's response.

Ariel looked back outside. They were hammering down the freeway through open shrub land that looked as though it bordered on an arid region in specific patches. "These location coordinates are really taking us out of the city, aren't they?"

"I know," Indya agreed. "But Ashley said to check in once we arrive. She'll be able to get a better GPS lock on the place and maybe help us with navigation."

"Maybe? That's 'encouraging,'" she commented sarcastically, less than convinced of their backup. "There were no real details in her missive."

Indya was silent for a moment, squinting into the horizon before she answered. "I think I know why. I'm unsure how else she would have convinced us to come to a ghost town."

Ariel frowned at the awkward statement, but as she followed Indya's gaze, she understood. Her heart fell through the floor as they approached. "What the hell is that place?"

"We're about to find out."

The settlement was nestled between the rocky outcroppings of two hills. It reminded Ariel of the doom towns built in the Nevada desert during the 1950s to test nuclear weaponry's blast impact. It was ominous. She sensed her sister's nervousness as well.

Indya parked the car on the outer rim of the hill, just off the road. She didn't want to be in sight of the town. The late afternoon sun was casting shadows that were perfect for allowing a clandestine approach.

The suspense made the small trek to the town pass quickly. Ariel and Indya found themselves skulking among the first buildings they encountered, sliding along the walls and beneath window sills to conceal their approach. Indya was leading the way, peeking around corners, before signaling for them to dash across roads and alleyways as they moved deeper in.

Ariel was sure they were at the center, and before her sister was about to move again, she gently grabbed her by the arm. "Indya, wait. Have you actually looked around? This place it's weird. It almost feels like it's abandoned, but yet I know it isn't."

"I know. I've been looking, trust me. I just kept us moving to get the layout of it all, in case Zoe loses contact. There are signs that people are still living here."

"But, where are they?"

"I don't know. This is not really the place I would expect to find research. Then again, I didn't know what to expect from his place. It's creepy as fuck."

"I think it's part of an illusion they wanted to create. You know, to divert unwanted attention."

"Then my question is the same as yours: where are the people?" Indya asked, looking as if the nerves were starting to get a hold of her.

Ariel looked around a corner and straight down the main road. "There's a big building down there that looks like it's a community center. The best answers could be at the hub of social activity."

"Your guess is as good as any."

Slipping between the shadows, the sisters found themselves just outside the building Ariel had pointed out. "I see an archway there. That must lead in. Let's be careful, okay? I... I feel uneasy. More so around this area."

Ariel nodded, swallowing hard.

The twins moved along the wall. They slowed; half-expecting to find someone near the opening, but it was as silent as the grave. With a single nod of agreement, both sisters looked inside. Their sight was filled by a massive garden courtyard, surrounded by an enclosed walkway.

"Guess we found them," Ariel mentioned, hearing her voice shaking.

Throngs of people were gathered in the open space.

Several things unsettled Ariel at that moment. The town, fairly average based on all outward appearances, had emptied itself of all its occupants—people who found themselves all gathered in that one place. These people—men, women, and androgynous individuals of all ages—wore mismatched pairs of clothing that would have given her the impression of homelessness in any other context. Yet, the most salient thing was that they stood motionless and silent while facing a large tower located at the courtyard's center. It was an eerie scene, and the tension in her chest threatened to snap at any second.

She jumped at the crackle of static and saw her ashen-faced sister adjust a receiver in her ear.

"It's Zoe," Indya said hoarsely. "She can barely establish a connection but says she is getting a better reading of the place. None of this appeared on any satellite image she could find. She says this building has the same layout as a prison. It's like a compound."

"There are no fences, no guards, and no measures of detainment. They don't look incarcerated to me. At least, not physically," Ariel commented.

"I see cameras," Indya pointed, indicating the randomly placed specs along the walls that surrounded the courtyard. "They look ancient, though."

"What's wrong with them?"

"I don't know. They look catatonic. I've never seen anything like this. This place is surreal. It just doesn't fit."

The courtyard inside was a vegetable patch, an orchard, and a communal hub combined. Small pavilions and pergolas had been erected, mismatched with the architecture that surrounded it. The entire garden seemed geared to support sustainable livelihood. An array of gardening tools even lay discarded at the feet of the entranced masses. It was as if someone had actually been attending to the grounds. All of them seemed as though they had been interrupted. Busy with some part of their day, before freezing in place. The sprinklers had been turned on, eerily pivoting from side to side, drenching the pants or leggings of those that stood close by, unmoving.

"They made a life here. Rather, I believe they tried. But I don't think they came here willingly. I think they've been left here to fend for themselves. Like they've been—"

"Forgotten," Indya finished. "But who were they

forgotten by?" Indya asked. "Their minds are as blank as their expressions."

Ariel felt slow to follow for a moment before recognition dawned on her. "Holy shit, I can't read them. None of them!"

Indya looked with slow and purposeful intent at her sister. "Ariel, it's the same block Jaydon has on his mind. The shape of it is the same."

Her sister was right. Whether because of their trance state, or some other inexplicable reason, they were inscrutable.

"Did you notice they're all marked?" Indya asked.

"No. They can't—" Ariel caught herself as she looked at them again. Her eyes moved from one figure to the next, and sure enough, she spotted a darker blemish behind the left ear of each one. "You're right. They all have it..."

Ariel heard the static again as Zoe tuned in, speaking in Indya's ear. She kept her eyes fastened on the silent crowd until she was done talking.

She noticed Indya look up then as if following an instruction. "Zoe says she is picking up a powerful energy reading. It's why the connection is so dodgy. She says it's off the charts." Indya was looking at the top of the tower. "Ariel, look up there. There is something at the top."

She did. She saw the sun reflected off the surface of something smooth yet faceted. It was nested among wiring and bent metal. Her senses numbed the longer she looked. She could tell Indya was experiencing the same until she eventually averted her gaze.

"What the hell is up there?"

Ariel never answered. She merely watched as the object flashed and emitted an otherworldly glow. It stung her eyes as it pulsed, bathing the area in a violent red. In that bloody hue, a hundred eyes fell on them—eyes devoid of will and even remorse. As one pair of feet shuffled, more followed until every mindless being in that space was turned to face them.

Piece by piece, in the midst of that horror, the clues slotted into place: The town in the middle of nowhere, the inconsistencies, the recurring mark, and the herd mentality. "Indya, I think we stumbled upon dad's experiments." A siren sounded, its long wail crushing the last of Ariel's resolve.

Indya barely managed to contain the panic in her own voice, "Then I think we've become variables in a new test."

The earth exploded as the mindless charged.

Ariel didn't hesitate as she grabbed her sister in a panic to run the way they had come. Using her ability, she tried propelling them forward, yet she knew her sister would never be able to keep pace. Fast as she was, her ability seemed almost useless in the face of the current danger. For her part, Indya could endure a fight with a few by healing fast. Against so many, though, she would indeed be torn to pieces. For once, they both were powerless.

The horde spilled out of the building like water from a burst dam. Bodies flowed in every direction. They were fast and were quickly minimizing the distance that lay between them and the twins. The buildings flew by as they charged out of town.

"Indya, we need the car keys! Now!"

Indya scrambled to extract the keys from her pocket as she ran behind her sister. Eventually, she held the wad out in a shaking hand and gave it to Ariel as they kept moving.

It felt like an eternity before they reached the car behind the hill. The experiments were still in pursuit. As they moved around to the doors, Ariel watched as some of them scrambled over the hill with inhuman speed, barreling toward them.

"Jesus Christ!" she said, launching herself into the driver's seat. Once inside, she thrust the key into the ignition and then turned. The car roared to life.

"I'll navigate! Drive!" Indya shouted.

A body catapulted onto the hood, and Ariel and her sister screamed as she slammed her foot on the accelerator. The car sped off, hurling the experiment against the windshield and to the side as it was shaken off. The way ahead was clear. As the engine roared, Ariel looked in the rearview mirror. In the cloud of dust left behind, she saw a line of figures scrambling to a halt, standing in a line as their eyes followed the retreating car.

The image seared itself into Ariel's mind as her heart pounded against her burning chest. She watched the needle of the speedometer climb.

"THERE, we have a map of the area." Indya was hammering away on the computer. They were back at the Den and gathering themselves from the terrorizing ordeal.

"How did you even manage to plant the location markers in the heat of the chase?" Zoe asked.

"I didn't. I planted them while we snuck in. We—is that a beer?"

Zoe's guilt was the sound of a bottle being opened and the metal lid clinking on the floor as it popped off. "For the nerves. For you, of course, but you can bet your ass I'm having one too. For the entire tech I geared you with, I've never felt so blind in my entire fucking life! What's up with that area? Here, drink a cold one while you talk."

Indya shook her head as she accepted the gift before answering. "The only clue I can give you is an artifact on a radio tower in the middle of that community square."

"The interference device?"

"It wasn't tech, Ash. If it was, it was unlike anything I've ever seen. It looked like a stone of some sort. But the place was surrounded. I couldn't get a good look. But, it may have caused the interference."

"And mind control," Ariel added from the side. She was still in a daze. The adrenaline felt like it had gotten the better of her.

The other two women looked at her, with looks of surprise mingled with concern.

"El, you've been quiet for a long time," Indya started. "I want to take a guess and say it's the shock, but you're too well composed for that."

"It isn't the shock. I'm over that. The drive was long enough to calm me down."

"Beer?" Zoe asked, holding out another opened bottle.

Ariel surprised even herself as she took the bottle by impulse, gulping down at least a quarter of it before setting it on a counter that she leaned on.

Indya simply stared at her sister with a hint of amusement. Zoe, in turn, offered a quirky smile and raised her own bottle, "Cheers."

"So," Indya started, "what's up then?"

"I was onto something right before all hell broke loose, and I completely misplaced the thought." Ariel was frustrated. She massaged her temples to concentrate. "There was something familiar. Something I had seen before."

"If there were something familiar in that zombie apocalypse shitshow you two-faced, then I've been the sidekick to the wrong twin here," Zoe said jokingly.

Even Indya smiled, but she was looking hard at her sister, sensing her jumbled thoughts. "Did it have to do with the experiments?"

"So we're sure they're test subjects?" Zoe asked.

"The way they moved, yes," Ariel answered. "And yeah. Something about them got me thinking before things got heated. Maybe if we could've read their minds, I could... Wait! That's it. We couldn't use our telepathy. That's exactly it. It reminded me of—"

"Jaydon," Indya finished, realization dawning on her features.

"Okay. Listen, you two need to stop finishing each other's sentences," Zoe commented. "I'm feeling super average here, and I'm usually the one to connect the dots."

Ariel continued, "Indya, he doesn't have the same mark, but you don't think..."

"That Jaydon could be an experiment?"

"Seriously!" Zoe interjected.

Ignoring her, Indya continued. "Ariel, if there is any truth to our hunch, and then Jaydon's entry into your life may not have been incidental."

Ariel didn't want to admit that to herself, but the connection started to dominate her thoughts. She whipped out her phone.

"What are you doing?" Indya asked.

"Calling him."

"Ariel, think about this before..."

"It's already ringing," Ariel answered bluntly.

Indya pursed her lips, and Ariel could see she was trying to hold herself back in commenting on her brash action. Her sister's palpable caution proved for naught. She lowered the phone from her ear.

"What? What happened?" Zoe excitedly asked.

"Nothing, he declined the call." Ariel simply stared at her screen. A few seconds later, a message popped through. She frowned, opening it to read. "He just sent me a text. He can't talk right now, but he'll call me later when he gets the chance."

"Thank god! That gives us time. Look, ballsy, as that was, we can't do stupid shit like that anymore. We need to reign in our emotions," Indya chided. "I'm taking a page from your book here, sis, okay? Ariel, do you hear me?"

"Yes! Alright, fine. Look, I just went on a whim before I flaked out and would be too scared to just do it. I need answers, goddammit! I need to know what crazy conspiracy we've been launched into. Jesus! It's been going on for years, and it feels like we've been twiddling our thumbs with other people's issues instead of looking at our own."

"I know, El." Indya gave her a solemn smile. Perhaps she understood more than she let on, Ariel thought. It was just hard to glean through the abrasive directness she some-times threw at people. "Truth is, we can't fall behind more than we already have. We're on to them now. And if we think about it that way, then this is no different from solving any other mystery. We're detectives, after all. Perhaps we'll fare better at approaching it like ones too. It's what we do best, isn't it?"

TEN

V and V

A DIFFERENT NECK OF THE WOODS

An entire day passed, and they were still no closer to uncovering more than they had the day prior. Indya had developed a headache from her sister's seesaw emotional state, and the fact that Zoe had kept the odd drink or two coming didn't exactly help. She had felt better throughout the morning, but her mind cleared noticeably as she put some distance between herself and the others. She had offered to get them lunch and was happy to take a drive into the city to catch a breather.

Fleetwood was still quiet. She had beaten the lunch rush, and she managed to beat the queue at a local deli to get them all a sub. She was in her car quicker than she expected. Not feeling up to facing the Den's drama, she decided she'd take a walk. Taking out her own sandwich, Indya jumped back out, left her car parked, and headed down one of the main avenues of a district that spearheaded the city's cultural scene.

For every person who was likely on the job today, there were at least three that seemed unhindered by any such obligations. The street cafés were packed, and talented buskers attracted sizable crowds for a weekday. Not that either she or Ariel could talk. They hadn't been to work themselves since the previous morning. They had merely called their assistant to indicate that they were working on their next case remotely and that research was taking up a lot of their time.

Indya went past all of them: the socialites, the rich, the unemployed, and the bored housewives. Eventually, she entered into a quieter section that bordered on one of the parks close to the city center. She stood there a while, hands in her pockets, contemplating whether she had the leisure of taking a stroll among the trees. She wondered if that would shake off the figures that had been following her.

She had noticed them the moment she had climbed out of her car. A hundred snap judgments passed through her mind before she decided on taking a walk, bringing her lunch along. If she was being followed, it was a simple invitation that suggested her vulnerability, and they had taken the bait. While walking through the music district, she had been uncertain as she lost her pursuer's psychic trace. For the next couple of streets, she had nervously scarfed down her sandwich while surveying her environment. Sure enough, she picked it up again. Whoever they were, they were close by, likely watching her at this moment.

Zoe answered the moment she sent a signal. "Indya? Did you confuse our menu requests?"

"Listen, Ash, I'm being followed."

There was a moment of silence while she heard rapid typing at the other end of the line. "You're on the edge of Fleetwood Park? What are you doing—?"

"No time. I need a lock and identification on the wolves on my trail."

There was another pause before Zoe answered. "I've

hacked into the security cameras of a few local shops and businesses on your path back to the car. But you'll need to wind your way through some of the buildings for me to be against the wall."

"Good. I'm on my way."

"Indya, I don't feel comfortable with this. Why not bolt for your car and just head to the Den?"

"They picked up my trail without any precedent the moment I set foot in the city. If I head back now without shaking them, then they're sure to follow. Besides, let's be smart about this. I want to end this hunt by gathering as much info as I can. Let's do this. You ready?"

Zoe sighed. "Alright. I'm set."

Indya ventured back in among the urban jungle and the predators in wait.

She sensed the alert spreading among them, and once she was in their midst, they prowled after her. Their psychic traces were peppered among the buildings, and she knew there was at least one of them within every two alleys that she passed.

"Fuck, there's a whole pack of them. Definite movement converging in your direction. Are you sure you just went to get lunch?" Zoe sounded a bit frantic.

"Yes. Where is it most congested?"

"Right now, they're at your back. But a few of them have charged ahead. Indya, it looks like they're about to pull out a double envelopment on you by coming from both sides!"

"A pincer maneuver? I'm going to stick to the main sidewalk. They won't dare—"

"They would. There is super little activity on for the next few streets. You won't be in public view."

"Ash, could you profile any of them yet?"

"No! Facial recognition is not picking up on any of them. I can't draw any personal information. It's like they don't exist. It's not for lack of clarity. Those cameras have given me full-on views on nearly half of them. There are just no records!"

"Shit. That's why they're so brazen. Change of plan. Time to get out." Indya picked up the pace, quickening her step as she approached the dining district.

"Indya! They're approaching from the front!"

Zoe didn't need to warn her. She saw them well ahead of time. Three casually dressed figures closed in from different vantage points on the street as she moved down the sidewalk. Their intent was as clear on their faces as it was from the thoughts she picked up through her telepathy. She had to act quickly.

A couple of feet ahead, she slipped into a corner café. As fortune had it, it was packed, and in the rush of lunchtime madness, she managed to slip underneath the countertop and straight into the small kitchen right at the back. The baker on duty was just about to protest before she bolted through, past the ovens, and directly through the back door.

She was in a narrow alleyway. A distance to her left, a fire escape ladder climbed the side of an apartment building.

"That was a good escape, but risky. You've cornered yourself."

"Watch me." She ran down the alley, reached the ladder, and started climbing. She was only a couple of rungs up before three pursuers barreled down the alley. She climbed faster, reaching the top just as the first was about halfway up. Once on the roof, she ran past air conditioning units until she reached the edge that sloped down the side of the building, facing an even taller hotel. She was about thirteen floors up in the air.

She climbed on top of the edge, looking up. This is absolutely insane, she told herself. Then again, she knew that actions executed in desperate times usually were. But it's been a while since I've stretched old muscles.

She leaped just as she heard shouts at her back. The superhuman lunge carried her across, and three stories higher, until she grabbed onto the railings of a hotel room balcony, surprising herself with her agility. Using her strength, she quickly pulled herself up, climbing over the ledge and onto the landing itself.

Below, at least four figures stood and watched with a mixture of awe and frustration. She fought down the impulse to smirk down at them and instead swung around. For a minute, her heart stopped as she considered that a locked balcony door would be a sore miscalculation. To her relief, she found the sliding door unbarred, slipped through, and closed it behind her.

There was no one in the lounge, but she immediately heard sounds emanating from the bedroom. Little was left to the imagination of what was happening inside. A discarded tie, heels, and other items were further evidence of what she had walked into. She tiptoed through the suite, heading straight for the door. She unfastened the lock, stepped into the hallway, and softly closed the door behind her. The amorous couple would be none the wiser. Standing there, she was reminded of a recent case she and Ariel had handled.

Taking a deep breath, she straightened herself, just as the concierge walked down the hallway. She acted as though she didn't see him until the last moment before looking up, smiling, and continuing to walk. He returned the favor without skipping a step as he headed down the hallway. She had infiltrated, but enemies waited at the gate. For now, she had time to plot before she reached the ground floor.

As she headed down, she purposefully used the stairs instead of the elevators. It gave her control of her surroundings, even if it was likely the first place they would think of looking for her if they got inside. She pounded down the steps, clearing floor after floor until she was at least ten stories down.

"Sorry, Miss You're not allowed down this way!"

Shit! Right above her, one of the housekeepers looked down with a heart-shaped face. "Sorry, I thought this was the way straight down."

"Oh, it is, Miss. But it will take you straight to the staff quarters. I think you took the wrong flight of steps. Why don't you take the elevator instead?"

Indya didn't know how she allowed the oversight, but she didn't think it wise to argue. "Oh, sure."

The housekeeper smiled. "Up here. It's right this way." Her face disappeared. Indya followed.

She reached the landing where the woman had stood, but as she looked down the hallway, the housekeeper was gone. "What the—?"

A figure launched from the shadows around the corner and pulled a bag over her head. The force of the action drove her downwards. As she was about to struggle, more dog piled on her, binding her arms and legs to prohibit mobility. Her screams were muffled by the bag, and she felt a hand land on her mouth over the coarse material to block the noise. "You best stop thrashing around," the voice whispered harshly. "It's for your own good."

"HELLO? Hello? Dammit, is this thing even—"

"It's working, Ariel. God! Trust me. I can hear you loud and clear."

"You guys really need to figure out some better tech, Zoe."

"Listen, using this enhanced radio frequency is the only way not to get tapped by today's standards. No one expects it. It's old but effective. The whole idea is not to be traceable."

"Forgive me for not jumping for joy, but that's the reason we can't locate Indya!" Ariel whispered harshly into the receiver.

"Ariel, I've apologized. I don't know how the hell I lost her. The only explanation I can think of is that she tested out acrobatics again. The impact of her landing damaged the transmitter. We faced a similar problem weeks ago."

Ariel was frustrated. The last thing they needed was to be one woman short in this operation. She careered down the district where Indya had been chased, deliberating her best course of action. "Where was the last transmission received from?"

"An apartment complex located right next to Guido's Café. She was cornered in an alleyway out back."

Indya wouldn't have been cornered by accident. If she was cornered, it was by intent. Ariel was wracking her brain to figure out the strategies her sister would have followed. She had to rely on her knowledge of Indya's personality alone, along with her sister's work ethic as a detective. Their mental connection only alerted Ariel of her sister's distress. Somehow, that connection was now severed.

Ariel reached the café and made her way around to the

alleyway. Stepping in, she saw someone leaning against the wall, smoking. With the smells of pastries and confectioneries wafting from an open door, she surmised that it was the baker.

The man raised his head as he blew a plume of smoke in the air. Looking her up and down, he frowned. "Hey! You're that crazy chick that charged through my kitchen. What are you doing back here?"

Being Indya's twin, it was all confirmation Ariel needed. She also read the memory as it surfaced in the baker's mind. Ignoring him to his dismay, she looked down the alley, noticing the fire escape ladder as the only means by which to slip away. She turned around, walking back onto the main street. She would have been on the roof, finding a way to get back to the main road to be in the public eye. Ariel's logic led her past the apartment block and down to the taller hotel building, separated from the apartments by another, although wider, alley. Hotel balconies arose a few floors above the apartment block's roof to offer a view of the city.

"Bingo."

"Having luck?" Ashley chimed in amid a jumble of wild static.

"Rhiannon Hotel. Can you access video surveillance?" There was no answer. "Zoe?" Her phone started to ring. Cursing under her breath as she looked at the display, she answered almost organically.

"Ariel, where are you? I need to talk to you."

"Jaydon," She closed her eyes, fighting back the emotion. "I'll call you back. Right now is not a good time." She hung up before he could respond. It took her a while to compose herself. She did not expect a call.

Right then, she felt a psychic outcry from somewhere

close by. Noises drifted through the side street that passed the hotel on its right. Intuition drove her forward, and she came around the corner just in time to see a white van. Suddenly a large hand came to rest on her shoulder, spinning her around. Her heart missed a beat as she looked into Jaydon's stern features.

"Now is the perfect time," he said. Putting his hand to the small of her back, he nudged her away from the alley opening and into the shadows of an adjacent building.

"Jaydon, let go of me. Now!"

He simply brought his finger to his lips in a gesture to keep quiet. "You need to be careful. If you don't cooperate, I'll have to use force. I will if I have to."

Before she could contest him, she heard a door bang open before two men emerged, restraining a smaller figure. The latter was shoved in the back of the van. Even with the face hidden, Ariel recognized the clothes. It was Indya, and she watched as the van's doors were closed, and the driver sped into and then down the main road.

She swung around as Jaydon's grip loosened and pummeled him on the chest, shouting. "We could have helped her!"

Jaydon grabbed her by the wrists, albeit gently, in an attempt to calm her down. "Ariel! Listen to me! Ariel! She'll be fine. You have to trust me."

"Trust you?" she asked in a hoarse voice, looking into his green eyes—eyes that had felt so life-giving but now made her feel dead inside. "You knew about all of this and still stopped me from helping!"

He pulled her closer while leaning in to talk to her. "You need to calm down. We're not out of the woods yet. Listen carefully. We are going to walk out of the alley, and head to the nearest diner to talk, where we can use other patrons as cover."

"You're mad if you think I'm going to—"

"Do you want answers about your father?" he asked her sternly.

Any retort died on her tongue. She simply stared at him, eyes glistening with frustration, and allowed him to pull her along once he started walking.

She felt numb when they were sitting at a table. Her sister had just been taken, and she was sitting in a run-down place where the frying oil overpowered the coffee that was brewing. She felt sick and baleful as she stared at Jaydon. She willed every bit of her psychic strength to tear his mind apart, but his immunity made her scorn feel worthless.

"It won't work, you know," he said, pulling a hand through his long brown hair.

"I get satisfaction from trying."

"I know you're pissed at me, right—"

"That's an understatement," she said.

He looked her in the eye, and Ariel saw him realize that he was not about to win. "Okay, then. I'll talk. I'm going to dump a lifetime of secrets on you in five minutes. So I hope you're ready." Her response was silence, so he continued.

"Twenty five years ago, your father was approached when one of his lectures in bioengineering gained traction. Interested in his radical views, a secretive division of the BBS approached him to work on the Alpha Project, which sought to biologically enhance human test subjects' genomes to display increased and even unique abilities. With the funding, the drive, and the alibi as a college professor—he achieved his first breakthrough: you and your sister. His first batch of super humans."

"Are you going to tell me anything I didn't know?"

"Like the fact that your father's alleged death wasn't an accident?" he countered.

Ariel felt her chest tighten, and she knew Jaydon could see on her face that he had her attention.

"In the ten years that your father covertly worked on their experiments, he made breakthroughs that none of the scientists in their employ could even fathom. They knew it, but so did he. So, your father went renegade. He became a potential liability if he could not be controlled. When it became desperate, they took control, the only way they knew how. By ending it."

"But he's alive," she said shakily.

"Their plan backfired. The vehicle he was driving had its brake fluid cut. They had called him into the lab, certain that he would perish once climbing onto the freeway. The car did crash, but he didn't die. He merely hit his head, which resulted in a severe concussion. Tracking the car, they knew of the wreckage before authorities did. They looked to see whether Gavin Vance was, in fact, dead, but he survived with no memory of who he was."

"What about my m—mother? Did she—?"

"Die? Yes. I'm sorry. The wreckage was set aflame. Any trace of the bodies or of what happened would have been undeniable. She was an unforeseen loss that burdened them with unwanted responsibility."

"Oh my God."

"But your father lived. His survival offered interesting collateral for the project investors by having his mind preserved—albeit not in memory. He was transformed into Sean Thompson, and this time they could yield rewards from making his scientific achievements public. But there was a problem."

His approach, if insensitive and pedantic, was somehow

calming her. "He could never recreate the super humans he once did."

"Yes. Test upon test was conducted, with hundreds of experimental subjects created. Some at their birth, some later in life. Only those subjects he worked on in his time before his involvement in AlphaPharm or BBS, assuming you know about them, were ever truly successful."

"You're one of them, aren't you?"

He hesitated before answering. "I was born or engineered, shortly after you became his greatest work—one of the original experiments when your father started. More of us followed although we didn't all display equally potent supernatural gifts. I have a few, but they're still unpredictable. At least we survived."

"What do you mean?" Ariel asked.

"Every experiment that succeeded us in your father's life as Sean Thompson often befell unfortunate fates. Many died or went mad, while the status of countless others remains unknown. As their research increased, and new technology became available to push the boundaries of science and nature, the methodologies and ideals that the Alpha Project wanted to run were becoming more unethical."

Ariel tapped her finger on the table, taking everything Jaydon shared and confirming based on what she had already found. "Your involvement with me was no accident, was it?"

His stony expression cracked as the shape of her question became more personal. "Many of us have been working together to ensure that the horrors of the past are not repeated. That requires both you and Indya's safety to ensure the corporation does not get their hands on you. If they should, their research will be fueled, and we have no doubt that it would transcend the inhumanity they have been guilty of." He paused, breathing deeply before continuing. "I was assigned to you. I just didn't think that I would come to care for you the way I did."

Ariel looked long and hard at Jaydon. She leaned over the diner's table, whispering, "If you really care for me, as you say, then bring back my sister." She waited a while before adding, "And help me find my father."

ELEVEN

V and V

LOST AND FOUND

She was shoved into a street, falling hard onto the asphalt. Her restraints were undone, and the bag was removed from her head. Indya's eyes stung in the overhead glare of the mid afternoon sun. Once they adjusted, she found herself back in a not-so-unfamiliar place that had been the theme of her nightmares the previous night.

She was back in Doomtown.

Behind her, wheels screeched as the van sped off and through a barricade that had been erected around the town. Where once there had been nothing, guards now stood to cordon off the area.

Swallowing hard, she looked around, and the once-abandoned town was now teeming with people attending to their run-of-the-mill bustle, imitating their own version of normality. In the commotion, some had stopped to stare at the new arrival. Pausing whatever they had been doing to look at her with curiosity.

"I'll be damned if I stay here," she said to herself. Her captors had made one mistake when they had grabbed her: they never patted her down. Acting as casually as she could not draw any more attention, she searched her person for the earpiece she had pocketed once the chase had gained momentum. Finding it, she popped it in her ear. The transmitter was still hooked on the inner fold of her t-shirt. The small light at its side was dim. Giving it a few flicks, it burned bright, and she spoke. "Ash, come in. The Fox is caged."

There was no answer.

"Ash, come in. Do you read me?"

"Indya? Oh, my God! You bitch! What the hell?"

She could not help but smile. "It's good to hear your voice, partner. They got me, but they didn't take all my teeth."

"Your tracker came online a couple of minutes ago. You were moving fast down the freeway that led to—"

"The fake town. Yeah. They brought me back to the compound."

"Listen, don't do anything hectic right now, okay. Your transmitter is about to go dead. I can see its battery is depleted. I need to keep an eye on where you are so that..."

The earpiece sputtered and then went dead, and Indya knew she was alone. She hoped her tracker would hold out if they decided to move her. This couldn't be the place they thought to bring her, she thought. They would have known that we found it.

"So, they finally found one of you."

Indya found the person who had spoken standing behind her and did a double-take. At once, she met with a voluminous head of dark hair that rose and fell in large ringlets around the woman's face. Her hair was streaked with grey. Indya noticed the lines around the woman's eyes and mouth. Indya would have judged her to be in her fifties. The woman was as tall as Indya, storm-grey eyes meeting her own. She was dressed in a loose-fitting ashen shawl, smudged with dirt, probably from the large community garden in the middle of town. She was at once familiar, even if a complete stranger, and before Indya could stop herself, she said, "Mother"

The woman cocked her head but soon realized what Indya had meant before offering a solemn smile. "I'm sorry, honey. I think you have me confused with someone. My name is Dahlia."

Indya hadn't invested much desire behind her suspicion, but it still cut deeply when it was disproved. "Oh. Sorry. I must have. Never mind." She looked down at her feet, fighting the sadness. She never realized how much she still needed to process. The thought was dispelled as another entered her consciousness. She didn't recognize it as one of her own. She looked back up into the woman's eyes. "Why would you think I'm an 'original.'?"

Dahlia's eyes widened and she gasped until her shock turned to awe, and she seemed to consider Indya anew. "You... you can read my mind?"

Indya realized that it was what likely happened. She was tentative but answered, "Yes."

Dahlia stepped closer, her voice lowering to a whisper. "Your ability you have control over it? How? What did our creator do differently on you?" She was scrutinizing Indya from every angle, suddenly marveling at her as if she was some otherworldly phenomenon.

Indya backed away ever so slightly. "What are you talking about? Are... are you gifted too?"

Dahlia looked around, suddenly mindful of her environment. Indya followed her gaze to the town barrier, where the guards looked too preoccupied to pay attention to the experiments walking around town. She turned back, motioning with her eyes to follow.

Indya followed the woman as she led the way down the street. She slipped between two buildings, beckoning Indya into the shadows. Indya felt reluctant but eventually conceded, moving into the gap herself. From beneath the pale fabric draped over the woman's shoulder, she removed an amulet. Its outer facets bore a ruby-red vibrancy, which deepened to a darker core at its center. Whatever stone was inlaid in the middle, it was unlike any she had ever seen.

A tension settled on her mind, as though a crown had been placed above her brow. A crimson veil drew itself over her eyes, bathing the world around her in red. She had been in this position before, experiencing a similar sensation when looking upon the stone atop the tower. She had neglected to mention it to Ariel in the madness they experienced. It was as inexplicable then as it was now, and she could feel her heart pounding frantically and the blood surging through her veins. She struggled to speak, the shape of the words almost uncomfortable on her tongue. "What is that?"

"You feel its power, don't you? It washes over you like torrential rain. It overwhelms you. Please, take it in your hand. "

"No, I don't—"

It was too late. Dahlia slipped the artifact into her palm, her fingers closing involuntarily around it. Her grip was hardly tight, but she felt the sharp bite of the stone's edge cut into her skin before feeling the warm sensation of blood dripping down her fingers.

"Rumor has it that the stone is the source of our fractured powers. Just like the stone, our magic is volatile and unpredictable. We were imbued with gifts that neither of us could use, yet we are haunted by them, controlled through them."

"Magic?" Indya asked incredulously. A strong part of her was in denial of everything Dahlia was positing to her. Still, she could not avoid the heat the stone emitted, starting to glow as her blood ran over its crystal facets.

Dahlia was cupping Indya's hands as they held the glowing amulet. So thrown was she by the entire interaction that she hardly noticed as the crimson had drained from her vision, revealing only the bright glow of the stone that now seemed awakened. "It responds to you. It recognizes you, the firstborn from its magic. It is as I suspected. You are an original. The magic that they sought to harness in their folly flows strongest through you! But this is wrong. Where is your twin? The magic convergence can only be achieved through the mutual ascension of the dyad."

The woman was crazed. Even in reading her mind, Indya could hardly make out a consistent thread of thought. However, what scared her most was that she could read the conviction that Dahlia vested in her words. Ludicrous as it was, she could not deny that a part of her might actually believe it.

A siren rang.

Indya threw herself against the wall, dropping the amulet to the ground. She felt a chill run down her spine. She looked at Dahlia, half-expecting her to go mad any second, but the older woman was as alert as she was. Dahlia picked up the amulet, peeking around the corner as shouts erupted from the barricade. Two men charged into view, and she was ready to fight for her life.

"Alpha they're here!" the one shouted. Indya recognized the voice to be that of one of her captors. She felt a vehemence begin to replace her apprehension, but what confused her was how he had reported the information to Dahlia.

"The girl must be protected at all costs. Take her. Hide her away until we have repelled them."

In the mere seconds that spanned their decision, Indya had delved through the minds of the guards. Realizing for the first time that their intentions toward her were not malicious as she first suspected. "I can help! Let me fight."

The two men looked at one another, then at Dahlia. She simply nodded, and they took Indya by the arms, ushering her away. However, as they brushed past Dahlia in that narrow space, Indya's hand reached out sneakily to pickpocket the amulet that was hidden among her tattered clothes. Feeling the stone in her hands, she cupped it tightly to keep it concealed.

As they rounded the corner, the sounds of attack increased while gunshots started sounding. The townspeople were in a state of panic, rushing into the nearest buildings to escape the chaos. Indya only got a glimpse of armored vans rushing forward to bolster the opposition. From this point of view, it was difficult to tell which side she actually belonged to. Before all this, her allegiance was merely to herself.

They slipped into a side street, running past many buildings until they entered one of the houses. The door was unlocked as they charged through. A brief look around told Indya that the home belonged to Dahlia. Before they guided her to the living room, she caught the most fleeting glimpse of more shawls hanging on the hooks by the door.

One of the men pushed the table away and then gave a mighty tug to slide the carpet from a trapdoor in the floor. He bent down to open it, revealing a dark crater.

Before Indya could oppose them, the man at her back

lifted her up and inside. She was swallowed by the darkness and then wholly enveloped as the trapdoor was closed and then locked. She heard the carpet slipping over the floor and knew that there was no way out.

After the men retreated, she listened intently for any noises in the aftermath of the attack. Yet, in that hole, no sound reached her. There was nothing but silence and shadow.

She waited. Then she waited some more.

After the quiet became deafening, a voice moaned from the darkness next to her.

ARIEL FELT COMPLETELY untethered from her surroundings. She was still sitting where Jaydon had left her as he stood up to answer a call. A day ago, his company was the last she would have imagined herself being in. She sagged in the diner's seat. Overwhelmed by the effort of trying to process all the information that he had shared. Fed up with the shaky relationships, she had invested her trust in and exhausted from throwing her weight behind the psychic burden of establishing a connection with her sister.

She still couldn't pick up a single trace of Indya's consciousness. Even when things had been tense between them, there had at least been a glimmer of her energy. There was none of it now. The twin pull seemed to be lost to the ether.

Jaydon had assured her that Indya was safe, that a plan was set in motion for her to be retrieved. Still, she was finding it hard to add credibility to the things he told her—especially when he claimed that he wanted to be the one to break the news. She perceived it as some twisted act of chivalry. His words were an aching fusion of disclosures and emotional confessions that, in her mind, blurred his true role in this saga. Why would he allow Indya to be captured if he promised to bring her back? Why separate the twins in the first place if they were both in danger? Why the secretiveness after so long that he had been involved with her?

There were too many unanswered questions and too little support to answer any of them. She wondered if Indya felt as alone as she did in that moment, wherever she had been taken. Did she feel as hopeless or as forlorn? Strained as their relationship had been over recent years, Ariel had felt bolstered by her sister's nerve and resolve. In the last few days, she also felt stronger, despite the instability that had crept into her life. Every memory awakened a pang of longing that translated into another psychic call left unanswered.

Jaydon returned but didn't take a seat as he hovered over the table.

Ariel simply stared into the empty space in front of her as she said, "I don't need to read your mind to know that you just got bad news."

"The compound Indya was taken to was just attacked. My people cannot find any trace of her. Renegade experiments were captured—ones that were not under the control of Project Alpha—but she was not among them. No one claims to have seen her. Ariel, I don't know if she was captured or managed to slip through their clutches."

Ariel didn't think herself capable of mustering any anger in her near lethargic state. Nonetheless, when the last fragment of his broken promise fell to the ground, she turned a fiery glare his way that melted his features in its onslaught. "You told me she'd be safe."

"I didn't premeditate this. We had accounted for all variables. I—"

"Let me tell you something about accountability. A promise is a deal that seals it, and before you make such an offer, you ascertain your hold on all possible contingencies. It is among the many formulas that have made both of us—my sister and me—great detectives. If you are telling me what you are right now, then you have claimed accountability without committing to it."

He was rubbing the back of his head to think, breathing heavily as his mind scrambled for the next right move. "We could go to the site. Perhaps if you used your ability then..."

"I can't read anyone's mind anymore, Jaydon."

"What?" he asked, the concern evident in his voice.

"You heard me. I realized it a few minutes ago while sitting here and trying to plot ways to get as fucking far away from you as possible. I'm surrounded by closed books that I never found difficulty reading until now. And it happened the moment Indya was taken by an enemy that you clearly didn't understand as well as you think you did."

Jaydon sat down before speaking in more hushed tones. "Ariel, I understand you're upset. But I'm on your side here."

"Then you wouldn't have allowed them to take her," she answered, leaning across the table to emphasize her words. "You stopped being on my side the moment you allowed that to happen."

She stood up before he could respond, and she charged out of the diner back onto the main street. She wasn't about to run. He'd only find a way to track her. He seemed reasonably equipped for that by now. However, she needed space, even though a bustling city street could hardly afford her that.

The hardest part about what she had done was that her relationship with Jaydon did not fade into the background in light of all else. Quite the contrary, it was front and center the minute he made himself a prominent part of a story that she was convinced didn't involve him, despite her sister's warnings. And there had been many. Indya had been skeptical of Jaydon's intentions the moment he communicated his love to her.

Ariel couldn't bring herself to admit whether she was the fool. Yet, the longer her sister's disappearance festered in her mind, the more plausible it became.

"Ariel."

Her head snapped up as the despondent trance she was in dissipated. Was it her imagination?

"Ariel"

Impossible, she thought, hearing the disembodied voice clearly the second time. She focused her remaining energy, keeping it poised for when the voice spoke again.

For a couple of long breaths, silence followed, and Ariel was catching herself before she got too excited.

"Ariel! I need you. Find me now!"

As the remnants of her sister's voice reverberated in her skull, Ariel rushed back into the diner.

WARM LIGHT SUFFUSED the basement as a match was struck, floating like an ember in the darkness. She could see the hand holding the match tremble as if the simple task was strenuous. Eventually, a wick was set alight inside a paraffin lamp, causing yellow light to wash through the small underground space. Behind the lamp, the light revealed the face to whom the voice had belonged. Even though she had already recognized it from a distant memory.

The light reflected from large lenses until the man pushed his spectacles back up his nose. A scruffy, short-cropped beard framed his strong jaw, lending some bulk to his lean face. His hair was untidy, if short, and his buttoned shirt drenched in sweat. His one hand clenched his side just below his ribcage. He winced in anguish as he tried to bring himself upright, with the color draining from his face in the effort. She could tell the pain was agonizing, even if she couldn't tell the nature of his wound.

Perhaps instinct should have propelled her forward to assist, but it was the last thing she thought about as she looked upon her father.

"Tell me this is a dream."

"If it is, I never want to go to sleep," he responded. He finally sat up but fell with his back against the far wall. He was breathing heavily, and it was clear that he needed medical assistance.

Indya still didn't move. Perhaps she had experienced her fair share of surprises of late, but this was the last thing she could bring herself to expect. Yet, unwillingly, something beckoned her forward, and her legs moved of their own accord. It brought her to kneeling beside her father. Beneath his shirt, there was a mark, almost like a burn, right over his heart. The longer she looked at it, the more she understood why she'd been drawn forward.

"You've worn the amulet."

He frowned, perhaps with good reason, she thought. They were strangers to one another, with ten years of mysteries lying between them. For those to have been her first words almost felt unfitting. But as he followed her gaze to the spot just below his neck, he understood. "A reminder left by something that contained more power than I initially thought. You've seen it?" he asked.

She simply nodded, remembering the force by which the stone had impressed its power on her and the fiery sensation it left on her skin. Initially, it had been a crushing pressure on the skull until it lifted to leave a clarity that she had never experienced. It was as though her mind had been renewed, and she was rediscovering her power. "Yes." She revealed the amulet she clenched in her hand.

"I can see that it was enough to leave you chan—urgh." He clenched his side, turning ghostly white as the blinding pain consumed him.

"You're hurt. Relax relax. Show me your wound. It's here, isn't it?" She reached out to gently lift his hand, seeing the cut and the darkened skin that surrounded what appeared to be a chronic wound. The veins that webbed around the pale skin were blackened, and she thought that he was suffering from blood poisoning. "Jesus, what the hell did you do to yourself?"

"I was reckless and desperate."

She lifted the amulet and held it up toward the light. It was then that Indya noticed the dried blood covering it, darker than her own.

Seeing how she noticed the blotched crystal, he said, "I needed to hide this before they found it, and I took some drastic measures. Despite my efforts, it fell from my possession."

Indya was appalled. "You stitched it inside yourself, didn't you?"

He nodded, sweat dripping down his forehead. "The amulet's energies were violent. It started to tear me apart from the inside. Raw and untamed, it can be volatile. I was a fool not to foresee the consequences."

Almost by impulse, Indya hovered her hand slightly above the wound at his side. He furrowed his brow in confusion, not knowing what his daughter was attempting until he winced in reaction when the flesh started to knit and weave together as it healed. It seemed to be working, but Indya felt that her own energy was being drained by the effort. After a short while, she had to desist, falling back as the action started taxing her.

For all that it was worth; it appeared to make a difference. The wound had not healed, but it seemed less malicious than it had been seconds ago. "Fascinating!" he whispered in an astonished whisper. "How long have you been able to do that?"

"Never. At least, not on anyone but myself. I tend to heal quickly. I didn't know I could project the power."

"Then, the amulet has started to augment your magic."

"Dad... I mean, Sean—"

"I was your father. At least, that is how I regarded myself, long ago, before things got out of hand. I do remember you. Why else would I know your name?" he asked, giving her an almost sad smile.

She could not bring herself to feel an emotional attachment to him based on an old memory, especially in light of recent developments. Instead of further broaching the issue, she asked a different question. "What is this amulet and the red stone set in the middle? I have seen it twice now. Once atop the tower, and once in the hands of one of your experiments."

"It is called the heart of Sekhmet—an ancient deity associated with warfare. She was greatly revered but also feared. Within her lie, the duality of both destruction and healing, powers meant for both protection and retaliation."

"You are a scholar of bioengineering. What interest did you possibly have in mystic artifacts and mythology?"

"Indya, we often don't know where our interests lie until we stumble upon them quite by accident. I didn't go looking for it. It was given to me by people whose initial intentions I took to be beneficent. I did not know what it would become."

"The ruination of innocent people's lives, perhaps? The interference with nature?" Indya fumed.

"Regardless of what accusations you throw at me to call forth my guilt, I could never deny the gift it gave me in you and your sister." He leaned closer then, before whispering, "I had thought your kind to be the future. I thought I could bestow your unique gifts on others—gifts that had the potential to shape the world for the better."

"Good potential is often abused," Indya stated bluntly.

"As I found out, perhaps too late," he solemnly commented.

"It is through this amulet then, that we gained our powers?"

"Gifts from the divine. Speed, strength, psyches that transcend space and time. All which could be used to the benefit or even the detriment of others."

"Are you telling me the latter was never your intention?"

He looked her in the eye as he answered; a serious and unflinching cast set upon his features. "Never. The people who unwittingly became the master of my career had a different view. Seeing the stone's properties, knowing what it could do, and realizing its reach in potency, they started to exploit its power. However, they needed me to bring their vision to fruition."

"Which brings us to where we are now. Do you realize

that an army of your creations are out there, controlled by this crystalline material—whatever it is—driven mad by its call, following the whim of whoever has it?"

"You must understand that I had no inkling of where they found more of the stone. Neither do I know how they propagated an idea to use it for the sake of mind control. However, whatever they had as raw material could never accomplish what the mystically imbued properties of the amulet could. It could not create super humans. Unforesee-ably, the substance in the stone was still similar, and it appeared as though scientific tampering could yield different results."

"And what did your scientific meddling yield? And how long did you tamper with the lives of others?"

He was silent for a moment, carefully weighing his next words. "There is one thing you must understand. By fusing science and the mystic arts, whatever I accomplished was a miracle in the earliest days. After the accident and after I became their celebrity, whatever followed was a deliberate series of mistakes on my part once I regained my memory. Once I remembered the atrocities they were planning."

"You are talking of the initiative known as Project Alpha?"

"It was more than a mere project. Alpha became a corporation all in itself, led by a megalomaniac. Their purpose was in creating a breed of bioengineered super humans."

"For what purpose?"

"I think you already know. You know what the amulet is where it came from."

Sekhmet. Destruction. Warfare. "They're creating a line of super soldiers."

He nodded. "To sell to the highest bidder."

"So all the failed experiments, the people who died or failed to show unique abilities, were the consequences of your purposeful sabotage? The amnesia never degenerated the knowledge of utilizing the amulet and the stone's properties. You merely kept it secret."

"I had too. You have witnessed firsthand what the corporation has done with their science and rudimentary grip on the powers of the amulet. If they were to tap into what I truly knew, there is no telling what the consequences might be. So perhaps it is time to allow others to use its powers that are better attuned to it."

She stared at the red depths of the stone for a long time, feeling her connection to it deepen. "Are there others? Others who are as powerful as Ariel or me?"

Her father held a faraway expression for some time before he answered. "There was one soon after. There was even a time when I thought I would have taken him in, as we did the two of you. But, your mother would not permit it. A young boy. Bright, resilient, even if reserved. He was the only one that didn't bore the two of you when you played as children. I think it was because you could never read his mind."

Could it be possible? Was he speaking of?

She never finished the thought.

"Indya. Indya!" The echo was hollow as the psychic call filled her mind. "Indya, I'm coming."

"Ariel?" She didn't understand. Their mental bond had never been this strong. Neither had their telepathic messages ever been this clear.

From the corner, her father perked up at the mention of her. "Your sister? Where is she? I would—"

He fell silent almost immediately as footsteps pounded on the floorboards above them, sending small particle of dust cascading down. She heard as they scrambled around the room above until the carpet was pulled back. Someone tugged at the trapdoor above them.

It couldn't be Ariel. She reached out, unable to feel the mental affinity of her sister anywhere immediately close by. She could sense her sister on the move, but not above her. Indya moved back, gripping the amulet tighter in her hand. Involuntarily she felt a shift come over her as her muscles coiled, and her vision flooded with red. A primal power charged through her, and she positioned herself for an attack.

Sunlight fell through the open hole as the door was ripped from its hinges. A voice called from above, directing others to go in while commanding that whoever was inside stand down.

Indya smiled, her muscles flexing as she read the uncertainty of the men about to climb down. They have no idea what they're facing.

TWELVE

V and V

ENTER THE GODDESS

"God, can you drive any slower?" Ariel asked, sensing the shift in her sister's psyche.

"You know, just when I think you two couldn't be any different at times, you do something that proves that you're exactly like your sister."

"Yeah, well, we take a page from each other's books every now and then. I still don't see you hitting that accelerator any harder, though." She knew exactly where they were going, and a part of her was apprehensive at returning to the terrifying Doomtown. Still, her sister was in trouble, and she knew that the place was out far enough that they needed to speed up.

It wasn't long before she saw the hills, and after that, the town that lay just beyond its ridge. As they approached, she immediately noticed how the defensive layout of the experiment's town had changed. A barricaded line seemed to have been erected, then shattered, and then raised again with more massive fortifications. Judging by the signs of destruction, it was no secret that it had been attacked.

"Dammit! Ariel, the area has been compromised. Project Alpha seems to have reclaimed it."

"How do you know it's them?"

"They have a special task force that bears very similar markings to the ones those men have on their vans. Ariel, I've seen them. They don't fuck around. We need to be very careful. Maybe we can still make a turn and approach from—"

"No. It's too late. They've seen us. They know we're here," Ariel said.

"How can you be sure?"

"I read their minds."

"From all the way here? They must be nearly a mile away!" he exclaimed.

"I can't explain it either, but right now, I'm not questioning anything that can give us an advantage."

"I thought you said you've lost your powers?"

"Ever since Indya reached out, they've been trickling back. I'm also starting to think that her psychic plea wasn't intended. She was surprised that I was on my way. Her thoughts only reached me because she was in distress. It was powerful enough that I was convinced she directed it. It must mean our connection is getting stronger."

"H—have you been talking to her this entire time?" Jaydon asked incredulously.

"Even going so far as plotting a plan. We may need to create a diversion."

Ariel guessed he shook off any further questions he may have had. "Okay, but big help that will be if they can already see us."

"They don't know who we are yet. We still have the element of surprise on our side."

"I hope you're right." He was tense. She still couldn't

read his mind, but his emotions wrapped themselves around him like an aura. Abstract as it was, it gave her a glimpse into his inner world that she never had before. Whether it was the manifestation of new power or merely intense perception, she wasn't sure. Somehow she was thankful that it was present at all. From it, she felt more trusting of him. Despite the lack of answers, she still had to hear many questions."

The car approached the edge of the barricade. As it rolled slowly to a halt, a woman walked around to Jaydon's window. Her jaw was clenched and her face stern, almost as if anticipating a fight. Reading her mind, Ariel couldn't blame her. She had been at the forefront of the latest attack. The adrenaline was still ripe in her veins. "Sir, this area is closed off. No one is permitted to enter. I'll have to ask you to turn around," she stated, sounding as militaristic as she was decorated.

Ariel was the one to give an answer. "We've been sent by Alpha's headquarters to survey the security measures implemented after capture. We received reports that one of your patrols found the town annexed from your control. Our job is simply to survey and see if it's been secured." Jaydon's mind was in a state of wild panic, even though his outward appearance revealed nothing.

The guard frowned. "They already sent a reconnaissance squad? They didn't inform us. May I see credentials?"

"Certainly." Ariel took out her wallet, flipping it open. She extended her arm past Jaydon to show it to the captain, who was called Ronan, she gleaned from the surrounding soldiers.

She nodded. "Alright then, I'll accompany you personally. Pull in your car over there, and I'll be with you shortly."

Nodding, Jaydon complied, rolling up his window and driving forward as a gap was made in the defenses. Once through, he turned to Ariel. "How the hell did you do that? The display sleeve of your wallet was empty. You had nothing in there to go on."

"Inception," she answered, without offering further explanation. "Aroused, the mind can become susceptible to a little perceptual tinkering."

Jaydon looked dumbstruck as he parked the car where they were shown, but he didn't ask any further questions. "I hope you know what you are doing."

"I don't. I'm figuring it out as we go along. It brought us this far. Just follow my lead. From the way you're acting, I sense you've done something like this before. You're a natural."

"Stop reading me, Ariel."

She smiled to herself. "You make it too easy."

They climbed out and stood beside the car, just as the Ronan approached. "I trust this inspection will be quick. We're planning a mass relocation of the experiments, so we need to plan logistics to start making that happen."

"Then let's get started. Take us to the central compound. I gather you've rounded them up in the courtyard?" It was the only place Ariel knew, but they had seen enough for her to see that it was a strong lead. It also happened to be in the direction of Indya's location.

"Indeed. More tasks teams are searching the houses as we speak. This way."

"Who are they?" Jaydon said, referring to the cluster of security that now added to their party.

"Our shield. Some of the test subjects get unruly if they aren't managed. "Now, shall we?"

They walked down the street, with the walled

compound straight ahead. Ariel knew her sister was close. One of these buildings had her trapped, and they were getting closer to discovering her. She was zoning in on her location when suddenly they were distracted by a struggle directly in front of them.

Two soldiers emerged from the courtyard archway, dragging a woman between them with a wild mess of hair. Ariel felt a pang at the familiarity of the woman's features. Still, despite wishful thinking, she knew the woman was not her mother. They threw her at the captain's feet.

"Dahlia. What trouble have you been stirring?"

The woman simply spat at her shoes, in reaction to which a guard hit her across the face to subdue her.

Ronan knelt, looking into the woman's eyes. "Now, I'll ask you again. What trouble have you been stirring? You've been hiding someone, haven't you?"

None of them could have foreseen what happened next. A street down, the windows to a house shattered, and men were thrown against the wooden frames on the inside. An amber glow filled the home as if an inferno had erupted within. Without knowing how she knew, Ariel was sure she knew where Indya was. But what the hell was that?

As one, their party rushed toward it, and the first among them kicked the door open. He was flung backward by a blast that left the air around them, feeling as though it had been ravaged by a hot desert wind. The captain was next, but instead of entering, she coaxed whoever was inside to come forward, pointing a gun at the door. "Stand down! You are grossly outnumbered. Come out and surrender. No one else will be harmed here today."

With the captain's attention drawn away, Ariel charged Ronan from behind, using her speed to create momentum to carry them over the threshold. They stumbled inside, but instead of falling to the floor, the woman recovered. Behind them, the other guards rushed forward to assist her. Still, Jaydon was on them, grabbing the first by the scruff of his neck and flinging him to the floor while whirling around to deliver a sucker punch to the one that came in from the side.

Inside, the woman lunged at Ariel, pushing her against the wall. She had the upper hand for a moment until Indya dragged the woman off her sister, delivering a decisive blow to the gut, causing Ronan to double over. The force of the punch launched an artifact from her fingers that fell and came to a screeching halt on the floor. It was still glowing, alive with an inferno beneath the stony face of the gemstone set in the necklace. It was inexplicable, but Ariel had no doubt that it was the reason for the blast that had rocked the house.

The equation shifted when two of the trackers who had come looking inside the house recovered. One whipped out his stun gun and jammed it into Indya's side to deliver an electric jolt. She let go of the captain, falling to the ground.

Next, he came for Ariel, but she was too fast. She dodged him, after which she used the force of his attack to launch him into the wall. Even though striking himself, he recovered, retaliating with another charge. It proved too slow once again, as Ariel ducked his attack with superior speed, bringing the palm of her hand up to crack against his jaw. The velocity of her hit proved intense enough to knock him back. He lost his footing and fell backward, rattled by the blow. Whether in pain or loss of consciousness, he didn't move.

She swung around to check on her sister, and sure enough, Indya was already stirring. Her ability allowed her to heal quickly from the effects of the stun.

Directing her attention to where the captain had stood

mere seconds ago, Ariel discovered that the woman had snuck off during the fight. To her dismay, she found the amulet was gone as well.

"Dammit!"

Indya stood up, feeling unsteady. "She got away, but she said she'd be back. She whispered in my ear right before she slipped away."

Jaydon charged in, looking roughed up and disheveled but nonetheless intact. "Ronan got away. The goons that were left standing followed. I don't think we have much time. They might raise the alarm."

"Then we have to think quickly," Ariel said. "Indya when you opened your mind to me you said that—"

"I found dad," she finished. "He's in bad shape, Ariel. Using the amulet, I could somehow enhance my powers and project my healing onto him, but only enough to keep him alive. We need to get him to a hospital."

Ariel's mind was racing. "The amulet. The inlaid stone is the same as the one in the tower, isn't it?"

"Yeah, I'm almost sure it is."

"Indya, you're connected to it now. I think you can channel its energy. I need you to tap into them now to activate the stone on the radio tower."

Ariel felt Indya reading her mind as soon as she mentioned that. Her eyes went wide. "Ariel, the experiments are gathered there what you're proposing—"

"I know."

Indya swallowed hard but simply nodded. "He's in the basement."

"Well, get him," Jaydon offered, slightly out of breath. "Meet us in the car."

With that, Indya sped off, with Ariel and Jaydon making their way down through the floor's trap door.

Propped up against the wall opposite them was the man that was their father, their creator, and right now, the man they needed to save. He wasn't doing well, and whatever healing Indya had managed seemed to be wearing off. His eyes were closed, and he barely registered them coming in. As she stepped closer, he whispered her name through a ragged breath. "Ariel."

"Ariel, he's in a lot of pain. Moving him might just send him over the edge," Jaydon said.

"We don't really have a choice. I'm going to try something. I hope it works." She reached out, touching his fevered head with her palm. Concentrating, she willed his mind to deep sleep. His mind was susceptible to his vulnerability, and his eyes shut firmly while his body sagged to the floor.

Jaydon rushed forward, pulling him up. Ariel was amazed. Jaydon was practically shouldering deadweight, but he managed to get her father to the opening. Ariel was out first, pulling up as he pushed, and with some effort, they got their father on the landing. Jaydon crawled out right after.

A few moments later, they were rushing out of Dahlia's home. For the time being, the street was dead quiet, and she was sure that they had been slow in raising the alarm. As soon as they turned the corner, however, the dynamic changed. The corporation's guards were charging toward their location.

A psychic ring went off in her mind, and she recognized it as coming from her sister. Looking around, she saw her standing in the distance, right in front of the compound wall. She was grounded in her stance as she concentrated. From this vantage point, Ariel could see the very tip of the tower coming alive as the red crystal pulsed. Its glow radiated outward, making it seem as though the walls had been drenched in blood.

All was silent.

In the moments that followed, her sister started to run madly toward them. The earth rumbled as hundreds of feet fell in unison, and the wave of bodies spilled forth beneath the compound's archway. From inside, she could hear screams sounding, even though the experiments were silent. She knew then that her plan had worked and that the experiments had turned on their captors. Looking to the front, she saw the soldiers given pause as they watched the advancing superhuman horde charging their way. A few ran, but others simply watched in awe.

Once Indya joined them, they rushed in the direction of the parked car. Jaydon helped her dad inside, not gently. Jumping in, doors slammed, and the engine roared to life as he sped away. Watching the chaos around them, Ariel could not help but reminisce on the last time they were confronted by such terror. Only this time, they caused it.

"This amulet did it do the same to you?" she asked her sister.

Indya, wide-eyed, looked at her sister and simply shook her head.

She didn't have to say much. Her mind was an open book. In their folly, the corporation had tried using their unrefined science to tap into the crystal's power. What was meant to be used as their weapon was now turned back upon them. Ariel knew Indya's experience was different.

Perhaps it was because she was engineered by Sean; maybe it was because the amulet's mystical properties worked differently. Regardless, they were dealing with a power that neither of them fully understood. As Jaydon drove right through the barricade to escape, leaving the corporation's stragglers to deal with the maddened masses, they saw firsthand how destructive it could be not to have the right knowledge.

ONCE BACK IN FLEETWOOD CITY, they arrived at the emergency entrance of the nearest clinic. Sean was attended to almost immediately and then wheeled off. Ariel stared forlornly after the medical personnel taking him away. She was irritated by her sentimentality. Concern over a man who hadn't been their father for a decade, but the emotions were there regardless.

They were taken to the reception area, and Indya dealt with the paperwork at Jaydon's direction. He recommended using a pseudonym, for the simple fact that his name as Sean Thompson held enough acclaim to merit unwanted attention. He sat with Ariel, not being clingy or invasive, but merely available. She didn't know if he was making his own deductions from her agitation, but in a way, she did appreciate his presence.

Indya returned. "The admin has been attended to. So is he. They say he is critical, but they're managing to stabilize him. I really thought that my healing had helped him more than it did," she said, hands to her hips and staring down at the floor.

"You did," Ariel answered. "I can tell. What I do want to know is how?"

"I'm not sure, El, honestly. One moment I was kidnapped, the next, I was back in that terror town, and then I was told of mystical artifacts used to birth power and enhance it once in existence. The first effect the trinket had on me was strange. It felt wrong. That is until I realized that it was actually 'cleansing' me before it made me stronger. I could suddenly hear more," she started, tapping her head, "feel more, and do things I couldn't do before. It happened the moment that stone made contact with my blood."

"She told us about that on the way. But, you didn't have that contact with the amulet, though?" Jaydon said, addressing Ariel.

Indya was the one to suggest an answer. "It's only a theory, but I think the moment my powers were altered, yours were as well. It may be because we share the same blood."

"Indya," Ariel began, trying to gather herself, "when we approached this woman—Dahlia's—house, there was a fiery blast that erupted from within. It nearly scorched us. Luckily we didn't stand too close. I could see that it roughed up the guy who recovered much later, though. Was that you?"

Indya nodded. "I'm still not sure how I did it either, but it was because of the amulet. It was odd, really. I could swear that I saw something in that light—a figure, with the head of a lioness. Crazy, I know. But what isn't at this point, right? Anyway, it was almost primal energy that filled me. I knew that if we were to win, I needed to use it."

"It's gone now, but can you still feel it?"

Indya concentrated for a moment, closing her eyes. "Yes, it's faint, but I can sense it. I think it's bonded with me. Which is strange because Dahlia had it for ages. And she's an experiment as well. I'd have thought."

"Dahlia isn't an original," Jaydon said. "If the amulet was used to create us as your father claimed, then our ties to it would be stronger—in theory."

"Ronan has it now," Ariel said. "I'm going on a feeling here, but I think it's crucial for us to get it back. I also believe that she wasn't merely a captain of the operation. She may have been posing, even using us to find Indya and the amulet. I just didn't read her mind to be sure. That was my mistake. But we can't just leave Da—"

"We have to. We have to trust that they can do what they can for him here. Without the amulet, we can't really channel my healing as potently. So we're just being idle in any case."

"Indya is right, Ariel," Jaydon added. "If your father's sacrifices are to be worthwhile, all those things he did to stall for time and prevent Alpha Corp. and their plots, and then we need to retrieve the amulet."

Ariel sighed. "Magic we're dealing with magic. What the actual fuck?"

THIRTEEN

V_{and}V

LITTLE BIRDS, MOLES, AND SOLDIERS

"You bitches have some hard explaining to do," Zoe said, throwing down her bag and keys on the counter.

"Ah, so this is the little bird that whistles in your ear when you're heading into danger," Jaydon stated.

"That's her," Indya confirmed.

Zoe looked from one to the other, seeming a little vexed, "Listen, asshole. You may be packing a big cock or whatever, but don't come into a women's den and call her a little bird."

He laughed, "Well, she is no nightingale."

Zoe scrunched her face, looking dumbstruck by his audacity. She looked at Indya. "What does he call you? Little mole? Did you honestly tell this guy everything about our operation and the kind of digging you did? And the fact that we basically broke into his security company?"

"To be honest, Ash, he started spying on us long before we even realized we were spying on him. FYI, refrain from those kinds of facts in the future before I've given you the full scope of the allies we bring in."

"Wait, that night in the server room. That was you?

Heck. I've been trying to find you forever," Jaydon said, amazed and amused.

"Well, here you are. We just bring our pursuers in amongst ourselves to spill the facts, you know. Very new age. But it's the modern style of espionage," Zoe commented snidely and with sarcasm. She was a unique flavor today, Ariel could tell. Then again, she had been in the dark for hours during the time the sisters got themselves into trouble. Her reaction was understandable.

"Listen, Ash," Indya began, "I need you and Jaydon to have a meet-and-greet, a reconnaissance, and an informational merger all in one. He is going to brief you on everything he knows about Alpha Corp. and any secrets that we might use to find chinks in their armor."

"Um are you serious?" Zoe responded.

Indya simply nodded.

"God, I need a drink. Okay, pretty boy. Settle in. Set up. Whatever. I'll organize some thinking juice." They walked off, leaving the two sisters to talk.

Ariel turned to her sister, asking, "Are you sure this amulet can turn the tide of this saga?"

"Yes. Look, we aren't really specialists in the mystical arts here. I get it. It's weird. Even dad didn't quite get it. I think a combination of research, smarts, ingenuity, and pure luck got him as far as it did. He stumbled upon a way to harness an ancient power. He didn't exactly break it down, except that it relates back to a goddess linked to warfare and destruction."

"Whoa, whoa. Okay. Just go slower. I need to process this."

Indya nodded before she continued. "So warfare, destruction. That spells bad news if Alpha Corp. gets their hands on it. They came close. You saw the stone atop the tower. I don't know where they found more of that crystal, but they didn't know what they were doing. Many of those experiments didn't turn out the way we did, Ariel. I think they tried finding ways to compensate for that. And it worked sort of. "

"Before they realized they couldn't control them." Ariel weighed the information in her own mind for a moment. "The Doomtown I think it was created to keep those experiments away from an urban environment. It wasn't just a dumping ground for failed experiments. It was a testing facility for the rehabilitated—in the sense that they had the makings of an army, once they figured out the kinks."

"If they get the amulet, they may be able to do just that. Did you ever wonder how dad got his injury?"

"No. How? I just assumed he was badly hurt in the fight or maybe even tortured."

"He was tortured, but it was self-inflicted. He hid that amulet from them. I think he's been doing it for some time. Once they were hot on his trail, he took some drastic measures. He cut himself open, to hide it under his skin. You saw the wound. I bet you can put together the rest."

"Blood poisoning and the wound never seemed to heal."

"Yes, but the amulet's power was also taxing him, harming him from within. It was literally killing him. His body rejected it, just as the amulet rejected him."

"If he was prepared to give up his own life to keep that thing out of the hand of the enemy, then more than ever, we need to be committed to getting it back."

"IT'S PRETTY IMPOSING, isn't it," Zoe commented.

"Didn't you break in before?" Jaydon asked.

"Break in is one way of looking at it. It was more like walking in. Obviously, there were just many doors to open."

"Well," he said. "They're all closed now. I can see they didn't need Elitelligence to cater for their latest security measure."

Jaydon was right. Though Elitelligence had dressed the BBS building in a gnarly attire of high-tech security systems, Indya knew nothing was entirely as impenetrable as good old manpower. Soldiers were lined around the entire complex. "Have anything that we can use against them going in?" She looked at her posse. "Information, that is."

"Some of my guys are inside. It's through them that we confirmed that Ronan and her squadron came back to BBS," Jaydon offered.

"I don't understand. Wouldn't they have ousted or even harmed your people once they landed at home base?" Ariel asked.

"Right before working alongside Alpha, I implemented measures to have my guys infiltrate their operations—posing as scientists, engineers, or general technicians. Like I said, they hired me for a reason. We know a trick or two. Even when we have to use it against our clients. Anyway, the place is heavily guarded."

"We did plan several routes to enter the building." Zoe took out a tablet. "Here is a blueprint of the institute, with all the entry and exit points plotted. I have to be honest with you, though—our options aren't looking great. Once inside, it's going to be a Marco Polo kind of shitshow as you try to outrun blind men."

"Have you hacked the cameras yet?" Indya asked.

"Pushy, aren't you?" Zoe retorted. "But yes, I have. Your target is, quite predictably, on the floor of your father's lab."

"Well," Indya said, taking a deep breath. "Let's figure this out. Every side entrance is blocked, even the bay area. There are virtually no blind spots, though we can maybe create one with some distraction. We can slip in with some effort, but whatever we do to create an opening will have them alert. If we're about to head up ten floors in a scenario where we need to plan and adapt every step, we cannot really afford to draw their attention. It's a catch-22. We have to choose between a potential fuck-up or a potential disaster. I'm going to need you by my side, K. We're going to have to use some old tactics and agency tricks to slip past their defenses."

"I say we go through the front door."

They were all left stupefied as they looked at her. Zoe smiled mischievously, Jaydon looked anxious, and Indya just seemed confused. Eventually, her sister was the first to speak. "Ariel, I don't know if the adrenaline is going to your head a bit, but aren't you the one that usually calls for caution? Especially in a compromised situation like this?"

"I'm going to reiterate this, merely because I still can't believe it myself. We're not just dealing with espionage, scientific scandals, and a web of lies spun by an elaborate oligarchy. We're dealing with magic. I stepped into all this very tentatively, merely because it progressively became too much to deal with. When this mystic twist set in, it just completely threw logic, conscientiousness, and planning right out the window." A laugh burst forth, perhaps involuntarily, as Indya tried to come to terms with this new side. Ariel was revealing herself. "Heck, it's already so batshit fucking crazy, I just say: fuck it. Let's go in, guns blazing."

It was an impressive speech—passionate, ballsy, wild, and utterly ridiculous. The more Ariel's words resonated, the more Indya bought into it. "I'm a bit rusty on my hand-to-hand combat training. You think we can take them?"

Ariel shrugged. "No better way than throwing yourself right into it."

"Okay, whoa. Ladies, the heat of the moment has made you stupidly brave. I get it. But, don't you think we need to be more careful about this?" Jaydon offered.

"I don't know. I like this dynamic. It's totally turning me on," Zoe said from the side. "Well, here goes. I'm going to create a diversion to the sides. Jaydon and I will find a way in. It should thin out the congestion in the front and give you a breather."

Jaydon sighed heavily, shaking his head. "You're all crazy. Every one of you. How are you even going to muster the strength to take them on?"

"Well, through the amulet. That bitch inside may have it. But Indya bonded with it, and per implication, so did I. I don't know about her, but I feel supercharged. Besides, I scoped the psychic vibe of the guys they have guarding the front. Burly as they are, the boys are shaking in their combat boots."

Indya gave her sister a grin. "Through the front doors?"

Ariel returned the expression. "Through the front doors."

FOURTEEN

V_{and}V

ASCENSION

The game was afoot as an alarm wailed through the night.

Having made her first move, Zoe nodded to the twins.

As one, the sisters emerged from hiding, falling into step as they walked toward the main entrance. Indya's heart pounded, and her fingers flexed in anticipation before curling into fists. The moment was upon them.

Whether because of shock or disbelief, the guards' response was delayed long enough for Ariel to charge at the nearest guard with inhuman speed. She left him on the ground as she ricocheted to her next target. On her turn, Ariel bounded over the steps to the men who rushed to attack her sister's flanks. Her fist connected with the jaw of a soldier who noticed her two late. His head flew back, and he fell unconscious from the jarring blow. Using the momentum, she stepped, turned, and then delivered a flying kick that sent the second guard flying into the glass wall of the foyer. The impact was hard enough for it to nearly shatter. Then it did, as Ariel threw another guard against it. The shower of glass rained down on the incapacitated men, and another alarm was set off.

More men rushed from the sides, albeit uncertain of their success in facing them. With Ariel's speed, none of them managed to fire a single shot. She disarmed them all, the force of her velocity sometimes even breaking the guns. At that moment, Indya saw the fiery tendrils that tailed in the wake of her sister's intense motions. She moved like a whirlwind set on fire.

Hearing a charge from the left, she spun around just in time as three more men launched themselves at her. She grabbed the first, spinning herself behind him as the second collided with them. It was enough for her to pull her fist back to land a punch while winding the man she was using as a shield with his sidekick's blows. As the third moved in, she detached herself, putting all her intention behind a spinning kick.

It exploded against his chest, sending him sliding backward. A psychic shockwave erupted from the impact, pushing back the other soldiers she had been dealing with. The attack caught even her off guard as she looked at herself, astonished by the amount of power that coursed through their veins. The amulet was calling them this close, and in doing so, it imbued them with unimaginable power.

Ariel rushed to Indya's side then. "We've taken care of quite a few, but others are moving in from the sides. We might as well draw them in and move closer to our target. That'll give Jaydon and Zoe time to slip into an unguarded entryway."

"Agreed. Let's move."

The lower floor was dominated by a cavernous reception area decked out with metal chrome and mirrors. Though the twins had no trouble telepathically tracing the direction of their advancing attackers, the reflective surfaces offered more than enough warning for them to prepare. It also showed them where the staircase was; once a squad rushed down to meet them.

Attempting to save time and curiosity about the limits of her power, Indya thrust a fist into a downward blow that cracked the tile floor. A wave of energy sent the guards off their feet. Before they could recover, Ariel was upon them. With quick jabs disabled them by hitting nerve endings to impact their mobility. That done, they didn't waste time running to the next level, hearing the voices of others pouring in from the entrance.

The ascent to the tenth floor wasn't more straightforward. As they hammered up the staircase, they were often faced with blind turns that suddenly brought them face-to-face with the enemy. Ariel, being faster, managed to evade sudden blows quicker than Indya could. In turn, Indya recovered more from hits that landed, maintaining the endurance and stamina needed to keep on fighting. Both had their weaknesses, both had their strengths. They were still consolidating new abilities and those they now shared with the other. Halfway up, they had established a rhythm and turned into a cyclone of destruction that decimated any opposition they faced.

Static crackled in Indya's ear as Zoe's voice came through, "Vixen, Vixen come in. We're in the building."

"Really? This isn't a military operation," Indya whispered in the microphone, breathless.

"Listen, with the heavy defenses we're going through, I beg to differ. Your buddy Jaydon here is a force to be reckoned with. He has cleared us a path all the way to the security hub. We've met his team here. We're about to throw the doors wide open. It will clear your path but also open others leading to you. You'll have nothing but yourself to rely on."

"Tell her to do it," Ariel said, still catching her own

breath as they stood on the verge of either succeeding or failing miserably. Indya had forgotten that her sister now had open access to her thoughts, including Zoe's report.

"Affirmative. We're ready. Head our way once it's done."

"Here goes, ladies."

A few seconds passed, and then every access door slid open along the length of the corridor they stood in. Every access pad installed on the lab doors flickered and then died, leaving the doors held by electronic locks swinging open.

Gathering themselves, the sisters moved down the corridor until Indya caught a glimpse of the familiar insides of her father's office. She skidded to a halt, and Ariel stopped next to her.

The office was empty but upturned. Filing cabinets had been pushed over and forced open. File upon file was tossed with their contents strewn across the floor. At the desk, drawers had been pulled out, with the insides ravaged. The computer was turned on. From the looks of opened documents, it was no mystery as to what the intruders had been after.

"I had thought they'd be here," Ariel said.

"They got what they needed. I think I know where to find them."

They dashed out and further down the hallway. The tenth floor laboratory lay ahead, and with its doors standing ajar, there was nothing to prevent them as they sauntered in. What they stumbled upon was horrific.

The entire layout of the laboratory was changed. Moving shelves were rolled roughly to the side, leaving glassware shattered and other tools scattered across the floor. On one of the counters, lab samples and equipment had all been shoved off. It had been turned into a makeshift operating table, surrounded by the masked, hunched figures of what Indya only assumed were the scientists in Alpha Corp's employ. Every face turned toward the entrance, regarding the unwelcome eyes that had stumbled in on their atrocious deed. In the middle lay a woman, her chest bloodied and torn. Surgical tools were lined like new murder weapons on the counter, just opposite. Hovering in the middle stood Ronan, amulet in hand, flanked by large guards to either side.

"What is the meaning of this?!" she spat. "Have I not given explicit directions that nothing is to deter us from what must happen here?"

"If you're talking about your regiment of guards spread thin throughout the building, then be assured that we gave them a warm greeting upon our arrival," Indya said.

"Enough. Detain them, you fools!" Ronan screamed, holding up one of the unrefined red crystals that she removed from her breast pocket. It glowed murderously red, and the lackeys at her sides reacted. Dark veins started cracking across their necks as the muscles tensed before they bulldozed forward through anything caught in the way, announcing their approach with what Indya could only explain as guttural growls.

"Uh oh," Ariel said. She stood at the ready as the first reached her. At first, Ariel dodged his swiping hand to grab her, but she proved less fast with the second. The experiment lifted her, tossing her over one of the counters until she came crashing down on the other side.

"Ariel!" Indya exclaimed, just as the other henchman reached her. Feeling the power of the amulet surging through her, she caught his hand as it came flying in but found herself only barely able to hold it from crunching into her face. She focused, channeling her psychic energy before pushing it outward and sending the experiment sprawling backward through her hands. He soon found his footing. Unlike the other guards, this man presented something more equal in power. Beating him would not be easy.

The other came diving in from the side but bent backward in agony just before he reached her. As he turned, reaching for his back, Indya could see metal tongs buried into the flesh, clenched against the bone of the shoulder blade. Behind him, Ariel stood, her dark hair hanging over her face as she breathed heavily. As the experiment thrashed about, the other came forward once more, this time swinging a fire extinguisher he had ripped from the wall.

Indya ducked and rolled out of the way just as it came down. Bursting open on contact with the force of the swing. A cloud of the dry chemical agent exploded forth, briefly concealing the brute. The twins used the opportunity to charge the group that surrounded the operating slab.

Ronan, noticing their approach, made a desperate play. "Move! Out of the way!" she shouted, worming her way in among the hunched figures who protested against the disturbance. She brought the amulet down, plunging it into the open ribcage of the test subject to pierce the heart. The effect was catastrophic.

The woman, as if resuscitated to life, sat erect. The howl of pain she uttered brought the people around her to their knees, hands over their ears as they desperately tried to block out the sound. The amulet emitted a searing glow, burning the woman's flesh. It was as if it was angry, rejecting the vessel it was being fused to. The lab began to tremble as the vibrations of power rocked their surroundings.

The woman looked over at Indya and Ariel, and with a

shock, they realized that it was Dahlia. Her wild hair framed a face in anguish. As the scream still rose from her throat, they could see her face cracking. Light burst through the broken skin as it strained to contain the power that coursed through her. Her skin started to burn, the pain leaving her body trembling before her head tilted back. The scream died as a blinding beam of light shot forth. It was as bright as the sun before the immensity of the power finally tore her body apart, leaving nothing but ash drifting in what appeared to be dying sunlight.

The force sent the amulet flying through the air before it clattered across the floor and came to a rest between the opposing parties.

Ronan, flung to the floor by the blast, didn't waste time to scramble to an upright position before running for the amulet. Neither did Indya. Channeling Ariel's speed, she propelled herself forward, grabbing the artifact long before Ronan could. No sooner had her hands closed around the stone than the full force thereof rushed through her. The amulet, bonded with her in blood, didn't resist. It subjected her to its full mystical might, spilling forth its godly power into her soul. Indya felt as though her blood was on fire, and she groaned in pain as she tried to contain it.

"No!" Ronan screamed, rushing forward. As soon as she touched Indya, she was thrown back by a psychic barrier, leaving Indya to wrestle with the immense power... until her sister was by her side.

Ariel kneeled beside Indya, feeling her agony more than anyone who was merely a bystander. She cupped Indya's hands as they clenched the amulet, unfolding them, before bringing her own hand down to replace the one removed. The amulet now rested between the twins' hands. A bridge between their wills, and the power that had filled one alone was split to course through them both. Indya's body sagged as the excess pressure was removed but still held her breath as the amulet imbued them with its magic.

Crimson light shone between their intertwined fingers, spreading through them as the last of the energies dissipated. Coursing through them, the power settled like a warm sensation radiating in their chests. All at once, it was over, and their arms fell to their sides. The amulet was gone, absorbed by the sisters.

Before the daze lifted, large hands restrained both of them. Ronan's goons had finally gathered themselves enough to prove useful again. The sisters were held fast by powerful arms and lifted to their feet. Reaching inside of herself, Indya still felt odd. Her sister mirrored her feelings. Something told her the power had not settled. On touching them, the guards made sure not to touch their skin, flinching as it burned them.

Ronan brought herself to stand before the twins. Indya would have thought she'd be fuming, but a malicious glee filled her eyes instead. "If I cannot have the power that I seek, then I shall draw it from you. I see no more fitting end than using Sean's very own creations in accomplishing what I set out for this company to do. Your bodies will give me all the secrets that I have longed for."

"Never," growled a voice. It was Ariel. Ronan spun around just as she lifted her head. Her eyes, at first closed, snapped open, and it was like staring into the sunlight. The force of her gaze made Ronan flinch, and the guards loosen their grip. Only Indya managed to hold the look. Ancient images flashed before her, of deities and times long past, until the swirling mass of mystic memories awakened the same energy within her. The sisters stood, a duality of the same ancient power, with Sekhmet's heart fused with their spirits. Fire danced in their eyes and on their fingertips, and they turned their terrible gaze upon the flinching overlord of the Alpha Corp.

The experiments, still squinting against the light, aimed to retaliate. The twins, like one, released a magical blast that obliterated both of Ronan's evil creations. Shielding her eyes, the woman moved back. The sisters could taste the fear on her mind while edging closer until she had her back against the wall. They looked upon the scene through their own eyes, the eyes of each other, and—touching the mind of Ronan—they could see themselves through hers. In that outer perception of themselves, they watched as their faces blurred before merging. A fierce goddess now stood in their stead. In its eyes were war and destruction and the only reserved judgment for the worst of souls.

The sisters spoke with one voice. "Look now upon the power once sought, and tremble in its wake. Your aim was to turn mortals into gods and turn gods into monsters. You have played with divinity without understanding it and committed crimes went disregarded. A lust for power begets blind judgment. In your devotion to that, face now its true consequence."

Their eyes shone brighter. Unable to avert her gaze, Ronan stared into the blinding light, her eyes turning cloudy the longer she watched. "No, no Please!"

It ended in an instant. The magic subsided, leaving the twins looking upon their blind nemesis.

"It's over," Indya said.

Jaydon and Zoe came rushing in, coming to a halt as they saw the laboratory's state. "Jesus," Zoe said, "seems like we missed the party."

Jaydon was awestruck by the scene but immediately struck by panic before he shouted. "Wait no!"

The sisters looked in the direction of his distress, seeing too late as one of the scientists grabbed a scalpel before charging Ronan and driving it into her neck.

Shock wracked the woman's body as her hand jerked up to staunch the blood flowing from the wound, but it was fatal. Helpless, they watched as the life drained from her face, blood streaming from between her fingers until her body crumpled to the floor.

It was a bitter end to a terrible fight, with each one of them firmly committed to leaving it forever behind them.

$\mathbf{V}_{and}\mathbf{V}$

VANCE DETECTIVES

Sitting at one of the only unoccupied counters in the Den, Ariel stared into space as her hands cupped her coffee mug.

"Your coffee is still hot?" Indya asked, taking a seat next to her.

Snapping back to reality, Ariel looked down at the steaming liquid. "Um yes. Why wouldn't it be? You made it fresh."

"Well, yeah. About an hour ago," Indya responded, looking confused. "I wonder—" She reached out before completing the thought, feeling her sister's hands. She winced as her fingers made contact. "It's like touching a stovetop right after cooking. It must be one of the side effects, I guess. Of the magic. No wonder."

Perhaps Ariel would have been more fazed about it a few days ago. Now, she merely shrugged before taking a sip of her heated drink. "Perks of the power, I guess."

"How are you feeling?" Indya asked. It was days since the invasion of the lab. It had ended differently from whatever they had imagined—and their imagination hadn't conjured up many alternatives, to begin with. After Ronan had been murdered by their own, all remaining decisions about their future course of action in the aftermath seemed mechanical despite their victory.

"The same as you, I guess," Ariel answered. "How do you respond to stuff like this? I guess I'm relieved that most of it is over. Alpha Corp. has been dismantled. Fleetwood City is safe from an unrestrained superhuman army. Dad seems to be pulling through nicely in his recovery. Things between Jaydon and me are better. We were lucky. I'm grateful. It was just I don't know. It was just..."

"Too much all at once?" Indya concluded.

Ariel nodded. "From all the things we found out of late, you don't just take that in your stride and move on. I'm feeling the effects of it trickling in as the days go by. I'm in a slump, I guess, despite our version of a 'happy' ending."

"Are you happy?" Indya asked.

"No. But, I don't think I'm sad either. It all happened, crazy and traumatic as it may have been. The ending really got me. It really hit hard." Seeing a woman killed had left both sisters stunned and dissociated. Perhaps, Ariel thought it had made what was to follow easier. Realizing that the Alpha Project's research could not be left unattended, they decided to destroy all traces of its violent history. By Zoe's guidance, they had instigated a fire before evacuating the premises. It was contained enough to cause the damage intended without burning the floor down. Emergency services rushed in to exterminate the flames, leaving the black mark on BBS's tenth floor. It was a bleak reminder of the mistakes inherent in leaving scientists unmonitored. The division of bioengineering had been terminated effectively until prompt investigations could be completed.

They would never find the answer. Jaydon and Zoe's combined resources and thinking erased all the case traces, including their involvement in it. In the minds of anyone unrelated to Project Alpha, it 'never happened.'

"There is a silver lining to this. The scientists who were in the lab that night confessed to a lot under interrogation. Jaydon managed to establish solid leads in tracking down others who have been experimented on. He has connected with many of them, and it snowballed into an increasing network as many of them came forward—even those presumed dead."

"I wish there was a way to reverse the effects of all the testing and experimentation."

Indya pursed her lips as she considered what her sister was saying. "Me too, but I saw Dad yesterday. We talked a long while. He said that the digital archives on his research would be sufficient to start developing solutions on a genetic level on a side track. He may not be able to remove the engineering. Still, he might well be able to reverse engineer it to lessen the damage. It would also stop any necrotizing effects that are still causing some of them to die." Ariel could feel Indya studying her as she talked about their father, looking for a reaction. "You know, you should really go see him. He seems invested in making things work between all of us. There is a lot of muddied water between us now, but he is willing to clear it."

"I'll open up in time. For now, I don't want to be around him alone. I've read your mind and caught a glimpse of what he's like. I'm not wholly comfortable with him yet."

"You know, sis, as much as telepathy offers you an insight to give you an advantage, vicarious thinking will leave you missing out on authentic moments. As much as we share, we're still different people. Things through my eyes may not be the way you see them yourself." Indya had calmed of late. Despite the flair, her personality added when she was more diplomatic and rational when the right moment presented itself. Ariel found herself surprised by her sister's take on things.

"Are some of these authentic moments related to your free runner stunts in the city?" Ariel teased. "One would assume that you'd use your newfound powers to better the city instead of jumping around it."

"Says the one practicing telekinesis in Fleetwood Park. You know you can just ask for a Frisbee partner, right?" Indya challenged.

"Oh, shut up," Ariel said, punching her sister on the shoulder.

"So, um, hey. I know things are still a bit sensitive and all, but I wonder if you're up for a mission." Indya asked.

"God! You're insatiable!" Ariel said, offering a laugh. "Already geared for action again?"

"Well, this time it really is altruistic. We haven't done anything about Doomtown or its residents. So far, it's the only bastion of the remaining traces of the Alpha Project. But arson isn't a solution with this one."

Ariel took another sip of her coffee, steeling herself for her sister's proposal. "Alright, I'm listening. What is it that you want us to do?"

"Well, since we're all a little high on magic and we're getting all jiggy with our powers—"

"Jiggy? I think your talks with dad have taken you too far back down memory lane if you're trying to make that work again."

Indya rolled her eyes. "Anyway, while we're playing around with our gifts, others don't really have the luxury. I was thinking we should start scoping out those with abilities powerful enough to garner attention. Maybe even guide them."

"From what I remember, the entire population of experiments there became supercharged powerhouses under the influence of the crystal. I think all of them have potential."

"Maybe we can play around with the properties of the stone then, with the amulet kind of gone and all," Indya offered.

"You're playing with fire, you know. It seems we've done that twice now, and the result has been pretty terrifying."

"We've absorbed the powers of the amulet now, though. With it, we may be able to awaken the raw crystal in a controlled way. Instead of using scientific interference, we tap into its power the way it's meant to—through some newfound mystic mojo. Something magical deserves to be handled by magic, after all."

Ariel wasn't convinced. There was more to this than her sister was letting on. "You're not telling me everything, are you? I can read you, you know. Even if you're trying to block me. You're getting better at it, but I can still discern something's up. What have you found?"

Indya looked sheepish as she tried to hide her guilt. "Well, I've been monitoring the place since Zoe bugged it. There have been some strange movements in and out of the town of late. One of Jaydon's guys actually did some reconnaissance. One of the men in town said that ragtag scout parties were moving just outside the border, never driving in. But that's not what's most alarming."

"What? What else is there?"

One of the men, called Jeremiah, reported to Jaydon's reconnaissance party that there have been some strange sightings at night. Dark figures in the distance, right on the edge of town. The last thing people see is the gleam of eyes before they disappear back into the night with inhuman speed. At first, it was only once or twice a week. But the sightings have become more frequent. One night, a little girl disappeared. When they finally found her, she was mute, only speaking after days. The things she said made the people lock their doors at night, with only a few brave enough to glimpse outside."

A part of Ariel went cold at hearing the ominous report, but another part of her felt ravenously curious. It left her with the pangs of reignited memories, to a time when things were simpler—when a simple mystery held enough 'magic' to make the spirit come alive. "Seems like an investigation is called for."

Indya grinned in anticipation. "Seems like a case for the Vance Detectives."

ABOUT THE AUTHOR

Renee Joiner has been in love with the supernatural for longer than she can remember, so it is no surprise that she is an author of paranormal urban fantasy. Although she discovered her passion for writing when she was only twelve years old, she didn't make her writing debut until many years into the future. Adventurous and fun-loving, she enjoys traveling to new places, exploring new sights and meeting new people. Thus, she delights in creating fantastical worlds that are sure to give her readers an escape from the real world while simultaneously providing thrilling entertainment.

Besides her special knack for writing, you'll also find a passion for metaphysics spirituality which she has been nurturing for over four decades. Renee hails from New York and currently resides with her husband in their empty nest —unless you count their three adorable fur babies—in Florida. She enjoys adding to her sea of knowledge and thus spends her free time learning new things.

To find out more about Renee Joiner, feel free to visit her **official website**.

facebook.com/reneejoinerauthor

twitter.com/iamreneejoiner

instagram.com/reneejoinerauthor

amazon.com/author/reneejoiner

SERIES BY RENEE

Thorne Sisters Chronicles
    Possessed by Magic
    Reincarnated by Magic
    Immortal by Magic

SIGN UP TO RECEIVE MY
NEWLETTER FOR ALL THE
LATEST UPDATES AND SPECIALS!

RENEEJOINERAUTHOR.COM/NEWSLETTER

Thank You..

Thank you for reading my book!
I really appreciate all of your feedback and I love to hear what you have to say. Please leave your review at your favorite retailer!